The Man in Lower Ten

by Mary Roberts Rinehart

TABLE OF CONTENTS

Chapter 1

I GO TO PITTSBURG

McKnight is gradually taking over the criminal end of the business. I never liked it, and since the strange case of the man in lower ten, I have been a bit squeamish. Given a case like that, where you can build up a network of clues that absolutely incriminate three entirely different people, only one of whom can be guilty, and your faith in circumstantial evidence dies of overcrowding. I never see a shivering, white-faced wretch in the prisoners' dock that I do not hark back with shuddering horror to the strange events on the Pullman car Ontario, between Washington and Pittsburg, on the night of September ninth, last.

McKnight could tell the story a great deal better than I, although he can not spell three consecutive words correctly. But, while he has imagination and humor, he is lazy.

"It didn't happen to me, anyhow," he protested, when I put it up to him. "And nobody cares for second-hand thrills. Besides, you want the unvarnished and ungarnished truth, and I'm no hand for that. I'm a lawyer."

So am I, although there have been times when my assumption in that particular has been disputed. I am unmarried, and just old enough to dance with the grown-up little sisters of the girls I used to know. I am fond of outdoors, prefer horses to the aforesaid grown-up little sisters, am without sentiment am crossed out and was substituted.-Ed. and completely ruled and frequently routed by my housekeeper, an elderly widow.

In fact, of all the men of my acquaintance, I was probably the most prosaic, the least adventurous, the one man in a hundred who would be likely to go without a deviation from the normal through the orderly procession of the seasons, summer suits to winter flannels, golf to bridge.

So it was a queer freak of the demons of chance to perch on my unsusceptible thirty-year-old chest, tie me up with a crime, ticket me with a love affair, and start me on that sensational and not always respectable journey that ended so surprisingly less than three weeks later in the firm's private office. It had been the most remarkable period of my life. I would neither give it up nor live it again under any inducement, and yet all that I lost was some twenty yards off my drive!

It was really McKnight's turn to make the next journey. I had a tournament at Chevy Chase for Saturday, and a short yacht cruise planned for Sunday, and when a man has been grinding at statute law for a week, he needs relaxation. But McKnight begged off. It was not the first time he had shirked that summer in order to run down to Richmond, and I was surly about it. But this time he had a new excuse. "I wouldn't be able to look after the business if I did go," he said. He has a sort of wide-eyed frankness that makes one ashamed to doubt him. "I'm always car sick crossing the mountains. It's a fact, Lollie. See-sawing over the peaks does it. Why, crossing the Alleghany Mountains has the Gulf Stream to Bermuda beaten to a frazzle."

So I gave him up finally and went home to pack. He came later in the evening with his machine, the Cannonball, to take me to the station, and he brought the forged notes in the Bronson case.

"Guard them with your life," he warned me. "They are more precious than honor. Sew them in your chest protector, or wherever people keep valuables. I never keep any. I'll not be happy until I see Gentleman Andy doing the lockstep."

He sat down on my clean collars, found my cigarettes and struck a match on the mahogany bed post with one movement.

"Where's the Pirate?" he demanded. The Pirate is my housekeeper, Mrs. Klopton, a very worthy woman, so labeled—and libeled—because of a ferocious pair of eyes and what McKnight called a bucaneering nose. I quietly closed the door into the hall.

"Keep your voice down, Richey," I said. "She is looking for the evening paper to see if it is going to rain. She has my raincoat and an umbrella waiting in the hall."

The collars being damaged beyond repair, he left them and went to the window. He stood there for some time, staring at the blackness that represented the wall of the house next door.

"It's raining now," he said over his shoulder, and closed the window and the shutters. Something in his voice made me glance up, but he was watching me, his hands idly in his pockets.

"Who lives next door?" he inquired in a perfunctory tone, after a pause. I was packing my razor.

"House is empty," I returned absently. "If the landlord would put it in some sort of shape——"

"Did you put those notes in your pocket?" he broke in.

"Yes." I was impatient. "Along with my certificates of registration, baptism and vaccination. Whoever wants them will have to steal my coat to get them."

"Well, I would move them, if I were you. Somebody in the next house was confoundedly anxious to see where you put them. Somebody right at that window opposite."

I scoffed at the idea, but nevertheless I moved the papers, putting them in my traveling-bag, well down at the bottom. McKnight watched me uneasily.

"I have a hunch that you are going to have trouble," he said, as I locked the alligator bag. "Darned if I like starting anything important on Friday."

"You have a congenital dislike to start anything on any old day," I retorted, still sore from my lost Saturday. "And if you knew the owner of that house as I do you would know that if there was any one at that window he is paying rent for the privilege."

Mrs. Klopton rapped at the door and spoke discreetly from the hall.

"Did Mr. McKnight bring the evening paper?" she inquired.

"Sorry, but I didn't, Mrs. Klopton," McKnight called. "The Cubs won, three to nothing." He listened, grinning, as she moved away with little irritated rustles of her black silk gown.

I finished my packing, changed my collar and was ready to go. Then very cautiously we put out the light and opened the shutters. The window across was merely a deeper black in the darkness. It was closed and dirty. And yet, probably owing to Richey's suggestion, I had an uneasy sensation of eyes staring across at me. The next moment we were at the door, poised for flight.

"We'll have to run for it," I said in a whisper. "She's down there with a package of some sort, sandwiches probably. And she's threatened me with overshoes for a month. Ready now!"

I had a kaleidoscopic view of Mrs. Klopton in the lower hall, holding out an armful of such traveling impedimenta as she deemed essential, while beside her, Euphemia, the colored housemaid, grinned over a white-wrapped box.

"Awfully sorry-no time-back Sunday," I panted over my shoulder. Then the door closed and the car was moving away.

McKnight bent forward and stared at the facade of the empty house next door as we passed. It was black, staring, mysterious, as empty buildings are apt to be.

"I'd like to hold a post-mortem on that corpse of a house," he said thoughtfully. "By George, I've a notion to get out and take a look."

"Somebody after the brass pipes," I scoffed. "House has been empty for a year."

With one hand on the steering wheel McKnight held out the other for my cigarette case. "Perhaps," he said; "but I don't see what she would want with brass pipe."

"A woman!" I laughed outright. "You have been looking too hard at the picture in the back of your watch, that's all. There's an experiment like that: if you stare long enough—"

But McKnight was growing sulky: he sat looking rigidly ahead, and he did not speak again until he brought the Cannonball to a stop at the station. Even then it was only a perfunctory remark. He went through the gate with me, and with five minutes to spare, we lounged and smoked in the train shed. My mind had slid away from my surroundings and had wandered to a polo pony that I couldn't afford and intended to buy anyhow. Then McKnight shook off his taciturnity.

"For heaven's sake, don't look so martyred," he burst out; "I know you've done all the traveling this summer. I know you're missing a game to-morrow. But don't be a patient mother; confound it, I have to go to Richmond on Sunday. I—I want to see a girl."

"Oh, don't mind me," I observed politely. "Personally, I wouldn't change places with you. What's her name—North? South?"

"West," he snapped. "Don't try to be funny. And all I have to say, Blakeley, is that if you ever fall in love I hope you make an egregious ass of yourself."

In view of what followed, this came rather close to prophecy.

The trip west was without incident. I played bridge with a furniture dealer from Grand Rapids, a sales agent for a Pittsburg iron firm and a young professor from an eastern college. I won three rubbers out of four, finished what cigarettes McKnight had left me, and went to bed at one o'clock. It was growing cooler, and the rain had ceased. Once, toward morning, I wakened with a start, for no apparent reason, and sat bolt upright. I had an uneasy feeling that some one had been looking at me, the same sensation I had experienced earlier in the evening at the window. But I could feel the bag with the notes, between me and the window, and with my arm thrown over it for security, I lapsed again into slumber. Later, when I tried to piece together the fragments of that journey, I remembered that my coat, which had been folded and placed beyond my restless tossing, had been rescued in the morning from a heterogeneous jumble of blankets, evening papers and cravat, had been shaken out with profanity and donned with wrath. At the time, nothing occurred to me but the necessity of writing to the Pullman Company and asking them if they ever traveled in their own cars. I even formulated some of the letter.

"If they are built to scale, why not take a man of ordinary stature as your unit?" I wrote mentally. "I can not fold together like the traveling cup with which I drink your abominable water."

I was more cheerful after I had had a cup of coffee in the Union Station. It was too early to attend to business, and I lounged in the restaurant and hid behind the morning papers. As I had expected, they had got hold of my visit and its object. On the first page was a staring announcement that the forged papers in the Bronson case had been brought to Pittsburg. Underneath, a telegram from Washington stated that Lawrence Blakeley, of Blakeley and McKnight, had left for Pittsburg the night before, and that, owing to the approaching trial of the Bronson case and the illness of John Gilmore, the Pittsburg millionaire, who was the chief witness for the prosecution, it was supposed that the visit was intimately concerned with the trial.

I looked around apprehensively. There were no reporters yet in sight, and thankful to have escaped notice I paid for my breakfast and left. At the cab-stand I chose the least dilapidated hansom I could find, and giving the driver the address of the Gilmore residence, in the East end, I got in.

I was just in time. As the cab turned and rolled off, a slim young man in a straw hat separated himself from a little group of men and hurried toward us.

"Hey! Wait a minute there!" he called, breaking into a trot.

But the cabby did not hear, or perhaps did not care to. We jogged comfortably along, to my relief, leaving the young man far behind. I avoid reporters on principle, having learned long ago that I am an easy mark for a clever interviewer.

It was perhaps nine o'clock when I left the station. Our way was along the boulevard which hugged the side of one of the city's great hills. Far below, to the left, lay the railroad tracks and the seventy times seven looming stacks of the mills. The white mist of the river, the grays and blacks of the smoke blended into a half-revealing haze, dotted here and there with fire. It was unlovely, tremendous. Whistler might have painted it with its pathos, its majesty, but he would have missed what made it infinitely suggestive—the rattle and roar of iron on iron, the rumble of wheels, the throbbing beat, against the ears, of fire and heat and brawn welding prosperity.

Something of this I voiced to the grim old millionaire who was responsible for at least part of it. He was propped up in bed in his East end home, listening to the market reports read by a nurse, and he smiled a little at my enthusiasm.

"I can't see much beauty in it myself," he said. "But it's our badge of prosperity. The full dinner pail here means a nose that looks like a flue. Pittsburg without smoke wouldn't be Pittsburg, any more than New York without prohibition would be New York. Sit down for a few minutes, Mr. Blakeley. Now, Miss Gardner, Westinghouse Electric."

The nurse resumed her reading in a monotonous voice. She read literally and without understanding, using initials and abbreviations as they came. But the shrewd old man followed her easily. Once, however, he stopped her.

"D-o is ditto," he said gently, "not do."

As the nurse droned along, I found myself looking curiously at a photograph in a silver frame on the bed-side table. It was the picture of a girl in white, with her hands clasped loosely before her. Against the dark background her figure stood out slim and young. Perhaps it was the rather grim environment, possibly it was my mood, but although as a general thing photographs of young girls make no appeal to me, this one did. I found my eyes straying back to it. By a little finesse I even made out the name written across the corner, "Alison."

Mr. Gilmore lay back among his pillows and listened to the nurse's listless voice. But he was watching me from under his heavy eyebrows, for when the reading was over, and we were alone, he indicated the picture with a gesture.

"I keep it there to remind myself that I am an old man," he said. "That is my granddaughter, Alison West."

I expressed the customary polite surprise, at which, finding me responsive, he told me his age with a chuckle of pride. More surprise, this time genuine. From that we went to what he ate for breakfast and did not eat for luncheon, and then to his reserve power, which at sixty-five becomes a matter for thought. And so, in a wide circle, back to where we started, the picture.

"Father was a rascal," John Gilmore said, picking up the frame. "The happiest day of my life was when I knew he was safely dead in bed and not hanged. If the child had looked like him, I—well, she doesn't. She's a Gilmore, every inch. Supposed to look like me."

"Very noticeably," I agreed soberly.

I had produced the notes by that time, and replacing the picture Mr. Gilmore gathered his spectacles from beside it. He went over the four notes methodically, examining each carefully and putting it down before he picked up the next. Then he leaned back and took off his glasses.

"They're not so bad," he said thoughtfully. "Not so bad. But I never saw them before. That's my unofficial signature. I am inclined to think—" he was speaking partly to himself—"to think that he has got hold of a letter of mine, probably to Alison. Bronson was a friend of her rapscallion of a father."

I took Mr. Gilmore's deposition and put it into my traveling-bag with the forged notes. When I saw them again, almost three weeks later, they were unrecognizable, a mass of charred paper on a copper ashtray. In the interval other and bigger things had happened: the Bronson forgery case had shrunk beside the greater and more imminent mystery of the man in lower ten. And Alison West had come into the story and into my life.

Chapter 2

A TORN TELEGRAM

I lunched alone at the Gilmore house, and went back to the city at once. The sun had lifted the mists, and a fresh summer wind had cleared away the smoke pall. The boulevard was full of cars flying countryward for the Saturday half-holiday, toward golf and tennis, green fields and babbling girls. I gritted my teeth and thought of McKnight at Richmond, visiting the lady with the geographical name. And then, for the first time, I associated John Gilmore's granddaughter with the "West" that McKnight had irritably flung at me.

I still carried my traveling-bag, for McKnight's vision at the window of the empty house had not been without effect. I did not transfer the notes to my pocket, and, if I had, it would not have altered the situation later. Only the other day McKnight put this very thing up to me.

"I warned you," he reminded me. "I told you there were queer things coming, and to be on your guard. You ought to have taken your revolver."

"It would have been of exactly as much use as a bucket of snow in Africa," I retorted. "If I had never closed my eyes, or if I had kept my finger on the trigger of a six-shooter which is novelesque for revolver, the result would have been the same. And the next time you want a little excitement with every variety of thrill thrown in, I can put you by way of it. You begin by getting the wrong berth in a Pullman car, and end—"

"Oh, I know how it ends," he finished shortly. "Don't you suppose the whole thing's written on my spinal marrow?"

But I am wandering again. That is the difficulty with the unprofessional story-teller: he yaws back and forth and can't keep in the wind; he drops his characters overboard when he hasn't any further use for them and drowns them; he forgets the coffee-pot and the frying-pan and all the other small essentials, and, if he carries a love affair, he mutters a fervent "Allah be praised" when he lands them, drenched with adventures, at the matrimonial dock at the end of the final chapter.

I put in a thoroughly unsatisfactory afternoon. Time dragged eternally. I dropped in at a summer vaudeville, and bought some ties at a haberdasher's. I was bored but unexpectant; I had no premonition of what was to come. Nothing unusual had ever happened to me; friends of mine had sometimes sailed the high seas of adventure or skirted the coasts of chance, but all of the shipwrecks had occurred after a woman passenger had been taken on. "Ergo," I had always said "no women!" I repeated it to myself that evening almost savagely, when I found my thoughts straying back to the picture of John Gilmore's granddaughter. I even argued as I ate my solitary dinner at a downtown restaurant.

"Haven't you troubles enough," I reflected, "without looking for more? Hasn't Bad News gone lame, with a matinee race booked for next week? Otherwise aren't you comfortable? Isn't your house in order? Do you want to sell a pony in order to have the library done over in mission or the drawing-room in gold? Do you want somebody to count the empty cigarette boxes lying around every morning?"

Lay it to the long idle afternoon, to the new environment, to anything you like, but I began to think that perhaps I did. I was confoundedly lonely. For the first time in my life its even course began to waver: the needle registered warning marks on the matrimonial seismograph, lines vague enough, but lines.

My alligator bag lay at my feet, still locked. While I waited for my coffee I leaned back and surveyed the people incuriously. There were the usual couples intent on each other: my new state of mind made me regard them with tolerance. But at the next table, where a man and woman dined together, a different atmosphere prevailed. My attention was first caught by the woman's face. She had been speaking earnestly across the table, her profile turned to me. I had noticed casually her earnest manner, her somber clothes, and the great mass of odd, bronze-colored hair on her neck. But suddenly she glanced toward me and the utter hopelessness—almost tragedy—of her expression struck me with a shock. She half closed her eyes and drew a long breath, then she turned again to the man across the table.

Neither one was eating. He sat low in his chair, his chin on his chest, ugly folds of thick flesh protruding over his collar. He was probably fifty, bald, grotesque, sullen, and yet not without a suggestion of power. But he had been drinking; as I looked, he raised an unsteady hand and summoned a waiter with a wine list.

The young woman bent across the table and spoke again quickly. She had unconsciously raised her voice. Not beautiful, in her earnestness and stress she rather interested me. I had an idle inclination to advise the waiter to remove the bottled temptation from the table. I wonder what would have happened if I had? Suppose Harrington had not been intoxicated when he entered the Pullman car Ontario that night!

For they were about to make a journey, I gathered, and the young woman wished to go alone. I drank three cups of coffee, which accounted for my wakefulness later, and shamelessly watched the tableau before me. The woman's protest evidently went for nothing: across the table the man grunted monosyllabic replies and grew more and more lowering and sullen. Once, during a brief unexpected pianissimo in the music, her voice came to me sharply:

"If I could only see him in time!" she was saying. "Oh, it's terrible!"

In spite of my interest I would have forgotten the whole incident at once, erased it from my mind as one does the inessentials and clutterings of memory, had I not met them again, later that evening, in the Pennsylvania station. The situation between them had not visibly altered: the same dogged determination showed in the man's face, but the young woman—daughter or wife? I wondered—had drawn down her veil and I could only suspect what white misery lay beneath.

I bought my berth after waiting in a line of some eight or ten people. When, step by step, I had almost reached the window, a tall woman whom I had not noticed before spoke to me from my elbow. She had a ticket and money in her hand.

"Will you try to get me a lower when you buy yours?" she asked. "I have traveled for three nights in uppers."

I consented, of course; beyond that I hardly noticed the woman. I had a vague impression of height and a certain amount of stateliness, but the crowd was pushing behind me, and some one was standing on my foot. I got two lowers easily, and, turning with the change and berths, held out the tickets.

"Which will you have?" I asked. "Lower eleven or lower ten?"

"It makes no difference," she said. "Thank you very much indeed."

At random I gave her lower eleven, and called a porter to help her with her luggage. I followed them leisurely to the train shed, and ten minutes more saw us under way.

I looked into my car, but it presented the peculiarly unattractive appearance common to sleepers. The berths were made up; the center aisle was a path between walls of dingy, breeze-repelling curtains, while the two seats at each end of the car were piled high with suitcases and umbrellas. The perspiring porter was trying to be six places at once: somebody has said that Pullman porters are black so they won't show the dirt, but they certainly show the heat.

Nine-fifteen was an outrageous hour to go to bed, especially since I sleep little or not at all on the train, so I made my way to the smoker and passed the time until nearly eleven with cigarettes and a magazine. The car was very close. It was a warm night, and before turning in I stood a short time in the vestibule. The train had been stopping at frequent intervals, and, finding the brakeman there, I asked the trouble.

It seemed that there was a hot-box on the next car, and that not only were we late, but we were delaying the second section, just behind. I was beginning to feel pleasantly drowsy, and the air was growing cooler as we got into the mountains. I said good night to the brakeman and went back to my berth. To my surprise, lower ten was already occupied—a suit-case projected from beneath, a pair of shoes stood on the floor, and from behind the curtains came the heavy, unmistakable breathing of deep sleep. I hunted out the porter and together we investigated.

"Are you asleep, sir?" asked the porter, leaning over deferentially. No answer forthcoming, he opened the curtains and looked in. Yes, the intruder was asleep—very much asleep—and an overwhelming odor of whisky proclaimed that he would probably remain asleep until morning. I was irritated. The car was full, and I was not disposed to take an upper in order to allow this drunken interloper to sleep comfortably in my berth.

"You'll have to get out of this," I said, shaking him angrily. But he merely grunted and turned over. As he did so, I saw his features for the first time. It was the quarrelsome man of the restaurant.

I was less disposed than ever to relinquish my claim, but the porter, after a little quiet investigation, offered a solution of the difficulty. "There's no one in lower nine," he suggested, pulling open the curtains just across. "It's likely nine's his berth, and he's made a mistake, owing to his condition. You'd better take nine, sir."

I did, with a firm resolution that if nine's rightful owner turned up later I should be just as unwakable as the man opposite. I undressed leisurely, making sure of the safety of the forged notes, and placing my grip as before between myself and the window.

Being a man of systematic habits, I arranged my clothes carefully, putting my shoes out for the porter to polish, and stowing my collar and scarf in the little hammock swung for the purpose.

At last, with my pillows so arranged that I could see out comfortably, and with the unhygienic-looking blanket turned back—I have always a distrust of those much-used affairs—I prepared to wait gradually for sleep.

But sleep did not visit me. The train came to frequent, grating stops, and I surmised the hot box again. I am not a nervous man, but there was something chilling in the thought of the second section pounding along behind us. Once, as I was dozing, our locomotive whistled a shrill warning—"You keep back where you belong," it screamed to my drowsy ears, and from somewhere behind came a chastened "All-right-I-will."

I grew more and more wide-awake. At Cresson I got up on my elbow and blinked out at the station lights. Some passengers boarded the train there and I heard a woman's low tones, a southern voice, rich and full. Then quiet again. Every nerve was tense: time passed, perhaps ten minutes, possibly half an hour. Then, without the slightest warning, as the train rounded a curve, a heavy body was thrown into my berth. The incident, trivial as it seemed, was startling in its suddenness, for although my ears were painfully strained and awake, I had heard no step outside. The next instant the curtain hung limp again; still without a sound, my disturber had slipped away into the gloom and darkness. In a frenzy of wakefulness, I sat up, drew on a pair of slippers and fumbled for my bath-robe.

From a berth across, probably lower ten, came that particular aggravating snore which begins lightly, delicately, faintly soprano, goes down the scale a note with every breath, and, after keeping the listener tense with expectation, ends with an explosion that tears the very air. I was more and more irritable: I sat on the edge of the berth and hoped the snorer would choke to death. He had considerable vitality, however; he withstood one shock after another and survived to start again with new vigor. In desperation I found some cigarettes and one match, piled my blankets over my grip, and drawing the curtains together as though the berth were still occupied, I made my way to the vestibule of the car.

I was not clad for dress parade. Is it because the male is so restricted to gloom in his every-day attire that he blossoms into gaudy colors in his pajamas and dressing-gowns? It would take a Turk to feel at home before an audience in my red and yellow bathrobe, a Christmas remembrance from Mrs. Klopton, with slippers to match.

So, naturally, when I saw a feminine figure on the platform, my first instinct was to dodge. The woman, however, was quicker than I; she gave me a startled glance, wheeled and disappeared, with a flash of two bronze-colored braids, into the next car.

Cigarette box in one hand, match in the other, I leaned against the uncertain frame of the door and gazed after her vanished figure. The mountain air flapped my bath-robe around my bare ankles, my one match burned to the end and went out, and still I stared. For I had seen on her expressive face a haunting look that was horror, nothing less. Heaven knows, I am not psychological. Emotions have to be written large before I can read them. But a woman in trouble always appeals to me, and this woman was more than that. She was in deadly fear.

If I had not been afraid of being ridiculous, I would have followed her. But I fancied that the apparition of a man in a red and yellow bath-robe, with an unkempt thatch of hair, walking up to her and assuring her that he would protect her would probably put her into hysterics. I had done that once before, when burglars had tried to break into the house, and had startled the parlor maid into bed for a week. So I tried to assure myself that I had imagined the lady's distress—or caused it, perhaps—and to dismiss her from my mind. Perhaps she was merely anxious about the unpleasant gentleman of the restaurant. I thought smugly that I could have told her all about him: that he was sleeping the sleep of the just and the intoxicated in a berth that ought, by all that was fair and right, to have been mine, and that if I were tied to a man who snored like that I should have him anesthetized and his soft palate put where it would never again flap like a loose sail in the wind.

We passed Harrisburg as I stood there. It was starlight, and the great crests of the Alleghanies had given way to low hills. At intervals we passed smudges of gray white, no doubt in daytime comfortable farms, which McKnight says is a good way of putting it, the farms being a lot more comfortable than the people on them.

I was growing drowsy: the woman with the bronze hair and the horrified face was fading in retrospect. It was colder, too, and I turned with a shiver to go in. As I did so a bit of paper fluttered into the air and settled on my sleeve, like a butterfly on a gorgeous red and yellow blossom. I picked it up curiously and glanced at it. It was part of a telegram that had been torn into bits.

There were only parts of four words on the scrap, but it left me puzzled and thoughtful. It read, "-ower ten, car seve-."

"Lower ten, car seven," was my berth-the one I had bought and found preempted.

Chapter 3

ACROSS THE AISLE

No solution offering itself, I went back to my berth. The snorer across had apparently strangled, or turned over, and so after a time I dropped asleep, to be awakened by the morning sunlight across my face.

I felt for my watch, yawning prodigiously. I reached under the pillow and failed to find it, but something scratched the back of my hand. I sat up irritably and nursed the wound, which was bleeding a little. Still drowsy, I felt more cautiously for what I supposed had been my scarf pin, but there was nothing there. Wide awake now, I reached for my traveling-bag, on the chance that I had put my watch in there. I had drawn the satchel to me and had my hand on the lock before I realized that it was not my own!

Mine was of alligator hide. I had killed the beast in Florida, after the expenditure of enough money to have bought a house and enough energy to have built one. The bag I held in my hand was a black one, sealskin, I think. The staggering thought of what the loss of my bag meant to me put my finger on the bell and kept it there until the porter came.

"Did you ring, sir?" he asked, poking his head through the curtains obsequiously. McKnight objects that nobody can poke his head through a curtain and be obsequious. But Pullman porters can and do.

"No," I snapped. "It rang itself. What in thunder do you mean by exchanging my valise for this one? You'll have to find it if you waken the entire car to do it. There are important papers in that grip."

"Porter," called a feminine voice from an upper berth near-by. "Porter, am I to dangle here all day?"

"Let her dangle," I said savagely. "You find that bag of mine."

The porter frowned. Then he looked at me with injured dignity. "I brought in your overcoat, sir. You carried your own valise."

The fellow was right! In an excess of caution I had refused to relinquish my alligator bag, and had turned over my other traps to the porter. It was clear enough then. I was simply a victim of the usual sleeping-car robbery. I was in a lather of perspiration by that time: the lady down the car was still dangling and talking about it: still nearer a feminine voice was giving quick orders in French, presumably to a maid. The porter was on his knees, looking under the berth.

"Not there, sir," he said, dusting his knees. He was visibly more cheerful, having been absolved of responsibility. "Reckon it was taken while you was wanderin' around the car last night."

"I'll give you fifty dollars if you find it," I said. "A hundred. Reach up my shoes and I'll—"

I stopped abruptly. My eyes were fixed in stupefied amazement on a coat that hung from a hook at the foot of my berth. From the coat they traveled, dazed, to the soft-bosomed shirt beside it, and from there to the collar and cravat in the net hammock across the windows.

"A hundred!" the porter repeated, showing his teeth. But I caught him by the arm and pointed to the foot of the berth.

"What—what color's that coat?" I asked unsteadily.

"Gray, sir." His tone was one of gentle reproof.

"And—the trousers?"

He reached over and held up one creased leg. "Gray, too," he grinned.

"Gray!" I could not believe even his corroboration of my own eyes. "But my clothes were blue!" The porter was amused: he dived under the curtains and brought up a pair of shoes. "Your shoes, sir," he said with a flourish. "Reckon you've been dreaming, sir."

Now, there are two things I always avoid in my dress—possibly an idiosyncrasy of my bachelor existence. These tabooed articles are red neckties and tan shoes. And not only were the shoes the porter lifted from the floor of a gorgeous shade of yellow, but the scarf which was run through the turned over collar was a gaudy red. It took a full minute for the real import of things to penetrate my dazed intelligence. Then I gave a vindictive kick at the offending ensemble.

"They're not mine, any of them," I snarled. "They are some other fellow's. I'll sit here until I take root before I put them on."

"They're nice lookin' clothes," the porter put in, eying the red tie with appreciation. "Ain't everybody would have left you anything."

"Call the conductor," I said shortly. Then a possible explanation occurred to me. "Oh, porter—what's the number of this berth?"

"Seven, sir. If you cain't wear those shoes—"

"Seven!" In my relief I almost shouted it. "Why, then, it's simple enough. I'm in the wrong berth, that's all. My berth is nine. Only—where the deuce is the man who belongs here?"

"Likely in nine, sir." The darky was enjoying himself. "You and the other gentleman just got mixed in the night. That's all, sir." It was clear that he thought I had been drinking.

I drew a long breath. Of course, that was the explanation. This was number seven's berth, that was his soft hat, this his umbrella, his coat, his bag. My rage turned to irritation at myself.

The porter went to the next berth and I could hear his softly insinuating voice. "Time to get up, sir. Are you awake? Time to get up."

There was no response from number nine. I guessed that he had opened the curtains and was looking in. Then he came back.

"Number nine's empty," he said.

"Empty! Do you mean my clothes aren't there?" I demanded. "My valise? Why don't you answer me?"

"You doan' give me time," he retorted. "There ain't nothin' there. But it's been slept in."

The disappointment was the greater for my few moments of hope. I sat up in a white fury and put on the clothes that had been left me. Then, still raging, I sat on the edge of the berth and put on the obnoxious tan shoes. The porter, called to his duties, made little excursions back to me, to offer assistance and to chuckle at my discomfiture. He stood by, outwardly decorous, but with little irritating grins of amusement around his mouth, when I finally emerged with the red tie in my hand.

"Bet the owner of those clothes didn't become them any more than you do," he said, as he plied the ubiquitous whisk broom.

"When I get the owner of these clothes," I retorted grimly, "he will need a shroud. Where's the conductor?"

The conductor was coming, he assured me; also that there was no bag answering the description of mine on the car. I slammed my way to the dressing-room, washed, choked my fifteen and a half neck into a fifteen collar, and was back again in less than five minutes. The car, as well as its occupants, was gradually taking on a daylight appearance. I hobbled in, for one of the shoes was abominably tight, and found myself facing a young woman in blue with an unforgettable face. "Three women already." McKnight says: "That's going some, even if you don't count the Gilmore nurse." She stood, half-turned toward me, one hand idly drooping, the other steadying her as she gazed out at the flying landscape. I had an instant impression that I had met her somewhere, under different circumstances, more cheerful ones, I thought, for the girl's dejection now was evident. Beside her, sitting down, a small dark woman, considerably older, was talking in a rapid undertone. The girl nodded indifferently now and then. I fancied, although I was not sure, that my appearance brought a startled look into the young woman's face. I sat down and, hands thrust deep into the other man's pockets, stared ruefully at the other man's shoes.

The stage was set. In a moment the curtain was going up on the first act of the play. And for a while we would all say our little speeches and sing our little songs, and I, the villain, would hold center stage while the gallery hissed.

The porter was standing beside lower ten. He had reached in and was knocking valiantly. But his efforts met with no response. He winked at me over his shoulder; then he unfastened the curtains and bent forward. Behind him, I saw him stiffen, heard his muttered exclamation, saw the bluish pallor that spread over his face and neck. As he retreated a step the interior of lower ten lay open to the day.

The man in it was on his back, the early morning sun striking full on his upturned face. But the light did not disturb him. A small stain of red dyed the front of his night clothes and trailed across the sheet; his half-open eyes were fixed, without seeing, on the shining wood above.

I grasped the porter's shaking shoulders and stared down to where the train imparted to the body a grisly suggestion of motion. "Good Lord," I gasped. "The man's been murdered!"

Chapter 4

NUMBERS SEVEN AND NINE

Afterwards, when I tried to recall our discovery of the body in lower ten, I found that my most vivid impression was not that made by the revelation of the opened curtain. I had an instantaneous picture of a slender blue-gowned girl who seemed to sense my words rather than hear them, of two small hands that clutched desperately at the seat beside them. The girl in the aisle stood, bent toward us, perplexity and alarm fighting in her face.

With twitching hands the porter attempted to draw the curtains together. Then in a paralysis of shock, he collapsed on the edge of my berth and sat there swaying. In my excitement I shook him.

"For Heaven's sake, keep your nerve, man," I said bruskly. "You'll have every woman in the car in hysterics. And if you do, you'll wish you could change places with the man in there." He rolled his eyes.

A man near, who had been reading last night's paper, dropped it quickly and tiptoed toward us. He peered between the partly open curtains, closed them quietly and went back, ostentatiously solemn, to his seat. The very crackle with which he opened his paper added to the bursting curiosity of the car. For the passengers knew that something was amiss: I was conscious of a sudden tension.

With the curtains closed the porter was more himself; he wiped his lips with a handkerchief and stood erect.

"It's my last trip in this car," he remarked heavily. "There's something wrong with that berth. Last trip the woman in it took an overdose of some sleeping stuff, and we found her, jes' like that, dead! And it ain't more'n three months now since there was twins born in that very spot. No, sir, it ain't natural."

At that moment a thin man with prominent eyes and a spare grayish goatee creaked up the aisle and paused beside me.

"Porter sick?" he inquired, taking in with a professional eye the porter's horror-struck face, my own excitement and the slightly gaping curtains of lower ten. He reached for the darky's pulse and pulled out an old-fashioned gold watch.

"Hm! Only fifty! What's the matter? Had a shock?" he asked shrewdly.

"Yes," I answered for the porter. "We've both had one. If you are a doctor, I wish you would look at the man in the berth across, lower ten. I'm afraid it's too late, but I'm not experienced in such matters."

Together we opened the curtains, and the doctor, bending down, gave a comprehensive glance that took in the rolling head, the relaxed jaw, the ugly stain on the sheet. The examination needed only a moment. Death was written in the clear white of the nostrils, the colorless lips, the smoothing away of the sinister lines of the night before. With its new dignity the face was not unhandsome: the gray hair was still plentiful, the features strong and well cut.

The doctor straightened himself and turned to me. "Dead for some time," he said, running a professional finger over the stains. "These are dry and darkened, you see, and rigor mortis is well established. A friend of yours?"

"I don't know him at all," I replied. "Never saw him but once before."

"Then you don't know if he is traveling alone?"

"No, he was not—that is, I don't know anything about him," I corrected myself. It was my first blunder: the doctor glanced up at me quickly and then turned his attention again to the body. Like a flash there had come to me the vision of the woman with the bronze hair and the tragic face, whom I had surprised in the vestibule between the cars, somewhere in the small hours of the morning. I had acted on my first impulse—the masculine one of shielding a woman.

The doctor had unfastened the coat of the striped pajamas and exposed the dead man's chest. On the left side was a small punctured wound of insignificant size.

"Very neatly done," the doctor said with appreciation. "Couldn't have done it better myself. Right through the intercostal space: no time even to grunt."

"Isn't the heart around there somewhere?" I asked. The medical man turned toward me and smiled austerely.

"That's where it belongs, just under that puncture, when it isn't gadding around in a man's throat or his boots."

I had a new respect for the doctor, for any one indeed who could crack even a feeble joke under such circumstances, or who could run an impersonal finger over that wound and those stains. Odd how a healthy, normal man holds the medical profession in half contemptuous regard until he gets sick, or an emergency like this arises, and then turns meekly to the man who knows the ins and outs of his mortal tenement, takes his pills or his patronage, ties to him like a rudderless ship in a gale.

"Suicide, is it, doctor?" I asked.

He stood erect, after drawing the bed-clothing over the face, and, taking off his glasses, he wiped them slowly.

"No, it is not suicide," he announced decisively. "It is murder."

Of course, I had expected that, but the word itself brought a shiver. I was just a bit dizzy. Curious faces through the car were turned toward us, and I could hear the porter behind me breathing audibly. A stout woman in negligee came down the aisle and querulously confronted the porter. She wore a pink dressing-jacket and carried portions of her clothing.

"Porter," she began, in the voice of the lady who had "dangled," "is there a rule of this company that will allow a woman to occupy the dressing-room for one hour and curl her hair with an alcohol lamp while respectable people haven't a place where they can hook their—"

She stopped suddenly and stared into lower ten. Her shining pink cheeks grew pasty, her jaw fell. I remember trying to think of something to say, and of saying nothing at all. Then—she had buried her eyes in the nondescript garments that hung from her arm and tottered back the way she had come. Slowly a little knot of men gathered around us, silent for the most part. The doctor was making a search of the berth when the conductor elbowed his way through, followed by the inquisitive man, who had evidently summoned him. I had lost sight, for a time, of the girl in blue.

"Do it himself?" the conductor queried, after a businesslike glance at the body.

"No, he didn't," the doctor asserted. "There's no weapon here, and the window is closed. He couldn't have thrown it out, and he didn't swallow it. What on earth are you looking for, man?"

Some one was on the floor at our feet, face down, head peering under the berth. Now he got up without apology, revealing the man who had summoned the conductor. He was dusty, alert, cheerful, and he dragged up with him the dead man's suit-case. The sight of it brought back to me at once my own predicament.

"I don't know whether there's any connection or not, conductor," I said, "but I am a victim, too, in less degree; I've been robbed of everything I possess, except a red and yellow bath-robe. I happened to be wearing the bath-robe, which was probably the reason the thief overlooked it."

There was a fresh murmur in the crowd. Some body laughed nervously. The conductor was irritated.

"I can't bother with that now," he snarled. "The railroad company is responsible for transportation, not for clothes, jewelry and morals. If people want to be stabbed and robbed in the company's cars, it's their affair. Why didn't you sleep in your clothes? I do."

I took an angry step forward. Then somebody touched my arm, and I unclenched my fist. I could understand the conductor's position, and beside, in the law, I had been guilty myself of contributory negligence.

"I'm not trying to make you responsible," I protested as amiably as I could, "and I believe the clothes the thief left are as good as my own. They are certainly newer. But my valise contained valuable papers and it is to your interest as well as mine to find the man who stole it."

"Why, of course," the conductor said shrewdly. "Find the man who skipped out with this gentleman's clothes, and you've probably got the murderer."

"I went to bed in lower nine," I said, my mind full again of my lost papers, "and I wakened in number seven. I was up in the night prowling around, as I was unable to sleep, and I must have gone back to the wrong berth. Anyhow, until the porter wakened me this morning I knew nothing of my mistake. In the interval the thief—murderer, too, perhaps—must have come back, discovered my error, and taken advantage of it to further his escape."

The inquisitive man looked at me from between narrowed eyelids, ferret-like.

"Did any one on the train suspect you of having valuable papers?" he inquired. The crowd was listening intently.

"No one," I answered promptly and positively. The doctor was investigating the murdered man's effects. The pockets of his trousers contained the usual miscellany of keys and small change, while in his hip pocket was found a small pearl-handled revolver of the type women usually keep around. A gold watch with a Masonic charm had slid down between the mattress and the window, while a showy diamond stud was still fastened in the bosom of his shirt. Taken as a whole, the personal belongings were those of a man of some means, but without any particular degree of breeding. The doctor heaped them together.

"Either robbery was not the motive," he reflected, "or the thief overlooked these things in his hurry."

The latter hypothesis seemed the more tenable, when, after a thorough search, we found no pocketbook and less than a dollar in small change.

The suit-case gave no clue. It contained one empty leather-covered flask and a pint bottle, also empty, a change of linen and some collars with the laundry mark, S. H. In the leather tag on the handle was a card with the name Simon Harrington, Pittsburg. The conductor sat down on my unmade berth, across, and made an entry of the name and address. Then, on an old envelope, he wrote a few words and gave it to the porter, who disappeared.

"I guess that's all I can do," he said. "I've had enough trouble this trip to last for a year. They don't need a conductor on these trains any more; what they ought to have is a sheriff and a posse."

The porter from the next car came in and whispered to him. The conductor rose unhappily.

"Next car's caught the disease," he grumbled. "Doctor, a woman back there has got mumps or bubonic plague, or something. Will you come back?"

The strange porter stood aside.

"Lady about the middle of the car," he said, "in black, sir, with queer-looking hair—sort of copper color, I think, sir."

Chapter 5

THE WOMAN IN THE NEXT CAR

With the departure of the conductor and the doctor, the group around lower ten broke up, to re-form in smaller knots through the car. The porter remained on guard. With something of relief I sank into a seat. I wanted to think, to try to remember the details of the previous night. But my inquisitive acquaintance had other intentions. He came up and sat down beside me. Like the conductor, he had taken notes of the dead man's belongings, his name, address, clothing and the general circumstances of the crime. Now with his little note-book open before him, he prepared to enjoy the minor sensation of the robbery.

"And now for the second victim," he began cheerfully. "What is your name and address, please?" I eyed him with suspicion.

"I have lost everything but my name and address," I parried. "What do you want them for? Publication?"

"Oh, no; dear, no!" he said, shocked at my misapprehension. "Merely for my own enlightenment. I like to gather data of this kind and draw my own conclusions. Most interesting and engrossing. Once or twice I have forestalled the results of police investigation—but entirely for my own amusement."

I nodded tolerantly. Most of us have hobbies; I knew a man once who carried his handkerchief up his sleeve and had a mania for old colored prints cut out of Godey's Lady's Book.

"I use that inductive method originated by Poe and followed since with such success by Conan Doyle. Have you ever read Gaboriau? Ah, you have missed a treat, indeed. And now, to get down to business, what is the name of our escaped thief and probable murderer?"

"How on earth do I know?" I demanded impatiently. "He didn't write it in blood anywhere, did he?"

The little man looked hurt and disappointed.

"Do you mean to say," he asked, "that the pockets of those clothes are entirely empty?" The pockets! In the excitement I had forgotten entirely the sealskin grip which the porter now sat at my feet, and I had not investigated the pockets at all. With the inquisitive man's pencil taking note of everything that I found, I emptied them on the opposite seat.

Upper left-hand waist-coat, two lead pencils and a fountain pen; lower right waist-coat, match-box and a small stamp book; right-hand pocket coat, pair of gray suede gloves, new, size seven and a half; left-hand pocket, gun-metal cigarette case studded with pearls, half-full of Egyptian cigarettes. The trousers pockets contained a gold penknife, a small amount of money in bills and change, and a handkerchief with the initial "S" on it.

Further search through the coat discovered a card-case with cards bearing the name Henry Pinckney Sullivan, and a leather flask with gold mountings, filled with what seemed to be very fair whisky, and monogrammed H. P. S.

"His name evidently is Henry Pinckney Sullivan," said the cheerful follower of Poe, as he wrote it down. "Address as yet unknown. Blond, probably. Have you noticed that it is almost always the blond men who affect a very light gray, with a touch of red in the scarf? Fact, I assure you. I kept a record once of the summer attire of men, and ninety per cent, followed my rule. Dark men like you affect navy blue, or brown."

In spite of myself I was amused at the man's shrewdness.

"Yes; the suit he took was dark—a blue," I said. He rubbed his hands and smiled at me delightedly. "Then you wore black shoes, not tan," he said, with a glance at the aggressive yellow ones I wore.

"Right again," I acknowledged. "Black low shoes and black embroidered hose. If you keep on you'll have a motive for the crime, and the murderer's present place of hiding. And if you come back to the smoker with me, I'll give you an opportunity to judge if he knew good whisky from bad."

I put the articles from the pockets back again and got up. "I wonder if there is a diner on?" I said. "I need something sustaining after all this."

I was conscious then of some one at my elbow. I turned to see the young woman whose face was so vaguely familiar. In the very act of speaking she drew back suddenly and colored.

"Oh,—I beg your pardon," she said hurriedly, "I—thought you were—some one else." She was looking in a puzzled fashion at my coat. I felt all the cringing guilt of a man who has accidentally picked up the wrong umbrella: my borrowed collar sat tight on my neck.

"I'm sorry," I said idiotically. "I'm sorry, but—I'm not." I have learned since that she has bright brown hair, with a loose wave in it that drops over her ears, and dark blue eyes with black lashes and—but what does it matter? One enjoys a picture as a whole: not as the sum of its parts.

She saw the flask then, and her errand came back to her. "One of the ladies at the end of car has fainted," she explained. "I thought perhaps a stimulant—"

I picked up the flask at once and followed my guide down the aisle. Two or three women were working over the woman who had fainted. They had opened her collar and taken out her hairpins, whatever good that might do. The stout woman was vigorously rubbing her wrists, with the idea, no doubt, of working up her pulse! The unconscious woman was the one for whom I had secured lower eleven at the station.

I poured a little liquor in a bungling masculine fashion between her lips as she leaned back, with closed eyes. She choked, coughed, and rallied somewhat.

"Poor thing," said the stout lady. "As she lies back that way I could almost think it was my mother; she used to faint so much."

"It would make anybody faint," chimed in another. "Murder and robbery in one night and on one car. I'm thankful I always wear my rings in a bag around my neck—even if they do get under me and keep me awake."

The girl in blue was looking at us with wide, startled eyes. I saw her pale a little, saw the quick, apprehensive glance which she threw at her traveling companion, the small woman I had noticed before. There was an exchange—almost a clash—of glances. The small woman frowned. That was all. I turned my attention again to my patient.

She had revived somewhat, and now she asked to have the window opened. The train had stopped again and the car was oppressively hot. People around were looking at their watches and grumbling over the delay. The doctor bustled in with a remark about its being his busy day. The amateur detective and the porter together mounted guard over lower ten. Outside the heat rose in shimmering waves from the tracks: the very wood of the car was hot to touch. A Camberwell Beauty darted through the open door and made its way, in erratic plunges, great wings waving, down the sunny aisle. All around lay the peace of harvested fields, the quiet of the country.

Chapter 6

THE GIRL IN BLUE

I was growing more and more irritable. The thought of what the loss of the notes meant was fast crowding the murder to the back of my mind. The forced inaction was intolerable.

The porter had reported no bag answering the description of mine on the train, but I was disposed to make my own investigation. I made a tour of the cars, scrutinizing every variety of hand luggage, ranging from luxurious English bags with gold mountings to the wicker nondescripts of the day coach at the rear. I was not alone in my quest, for the girl in blue was just ahead of me. Car by car she preceded me through the train, unconscious that I was behind her, looking at each passenger as she passed. I fancied the proceeding was distasteful, but that she had determined on a course and was carrying it through. We reached the end of the train almost together—empty-handed, both of us.

The girl went out to the platform. When she saw me she moved aside, and I stepped out beside her. Behind us the track curved sharply; the early sunshine threw the train, in long black shadow, over the hot earth. Forward somewhere they were hammering. The girl said nothing, but her profile was strained and anxious.

"I—if you have lost anything," I began, "I wish you would let me try to help. Not that my own success is anything to boast of."

She hardly glanced at me. It was not flattering. "I have not been robbed, if that is what you mean," she replied quietly. "I am—perplexed. That is all."

There was nothing to say to that. I lifted my hat—the other fellow's hat—and turned to go back to my car. Two or three members of the train crew, including the conductor, were standing in the shadow talking. And at that moment, from a farm-house near came the swift clang of the breakfast bell, calling in the hands from barn and pasture. I turned back to the girl.

"We may be here for an hour," I said, "and there is no buffet car on. If I remember my youth, that bell means ham and eggs and country butter and coffee. If you care to run the risk—"

"I am not hungry," she said, "but perhaps a cup of coffee—dear me, I believe I am hungry," she finished. "Only—" She glanced back of her.

"I can bring your companion," I suggested, without enthusiasm. But the young woman shook her head.

"She is not hungry," she objected, "and she is very—well, I know she wouldn't come. Do you suppose we could make it if we run?"

"I haven't any idea," I said cheerfully. "Any old train would be better than this one, if it does leave us behind."

"Yes. Any train would be better than this one," she repeated gravely. I found myself watching her changing expression. I had spoken two dozen words to her and already I felt that I knew the lights and shades in her voice,—I, who had always known how a woman rode to hounds, and who never could have told the color of her hair.

I stepped down on the ties and turned to assist her, and together we walked back to where the conductor and the porter from our car were in close conversation. Instinctively my hand went to my cigarette pocket and came out empty. She saw the gesture.

"If you want to smoke, you may," she said. "I have a big cousin who smokes all the time. He says I am 'kippered.'"

I drew out the gun-metal cigarette case and opened it. But this most commonplace action had an extraordinary result: the girl beside me stopped dead still and stood staring at it with fascinated eyes.

"Is—where did you get that?" she demanded, with a catch in her voice; her gaze still fixed on the cigarette case.

"Then you haven't heard the rest of the tragedy?" I asked, holding out the case. "It's frightfully bad luck for me, but it makes a good story. You see—"

At that moment the conductor and porter ceased their colloquy. The conductor came directly toward me, tugging as he came at his bristling gray mustache.

"I would like to talk to you in the car," he said to me, with a curious glance at the young lady.

"Can't it wait?" I objected. "We are on our way to a cup of coffee and a slice of bacon. Be merciful, as you are powerful."

"I'm afraid the breakfast will have to wait," he replied. "I won't keep you long." There was a note of authority in his voice which I resented; but, after all, the circumstances were unusual.

"We'll have to defer that cup of coffee for a while," I said to the girl; "but don't despair; there's breakfast somewhere."

As we entered the car, she stood aside, but I felt rather than saw that she followed us. I was surprised to see a half dozen men gathered around the berth in which I had wakened, number seven. It had not yet been made up.

As we passed along the aisle, I was conscious of a new expression on the faces of the passengers. The tall woman who had fainted was searching my face with narrowed eyes, while the stout woman of the kindly heart avoided my gaze, and pretended to look out the window.

As we pushed our way through the group, I fancied that it closed around me ominously. The conductor said nothing, but led the way without ceremony to the side of the berth.

"What's the matter?" I inquired. I was puzzled, but not apprehensive. "Have you some of my things? I'd be thankful even for my shoes; these are confoundedly tight."

Nobody spoke, and I fell silent, too. For one of the pillows had been turned over, and the under side of the white case was streaked with brownish stains. I think it was a perceptible time before I realized that the stains were blood, and that the faces around were filled with suspicion and distrust.

"Why, it—that looks like blood," I said vacuously. There was an incessant pounding in my ears, and the conductor's voice came from far off.

"It is blood," he asserted grimly.

I looked around with a dizzy attempt at nonchalance. "Even if it is," I remonstrated, "surely you don't suppose for a moment that I know anything about it!"

The amateur detective elbowed his way in. He had a scrap of transparent paper in his hand, and a pencil.

"I would like permission to trace the stains," he began eagerly. "Also"—to me—"if you will kindly jab your finger with a pin—needle—anything—"

"If you don't keep out of this," the conductor said savagely, "I will do some jabbing myself. As for you, sir—" he turned to me. I was absolutely innocent, but I knew that I presented a typical picture of guilt; I was covered with cold sweat, and the pounding in my ears kept up dizzily. "As for you, sir—"

The irrepressible amateur detective made a quick pounce at the pillow and pushed back the cover. Before our incredulous eyes he drew out a narrow steel dirk which had been buried to the small cross that served as a head.

There was a chorus of voices around, a quick surging forward of the crowd. So that was what had scratched my hand! I buried the wound in my coat pocket.

"Well," I said, trying to speak naturally, "doesn't that prove what I have been telling you? The man who committed the murder belonged to this berth, and made an exchange in some way after the crime. How do you know he didn't change the tags so I would come back to this berth?" This was an inspiration; I was pleased with it. "That's what he did, he changed the tags," I reiterated.

There was a murmur of assent around. The doctor, who was standing beside me, put his hand on my arm. "If this gentleman committed this crime, and I for one feel sure he did not, then who is the fellow who got away? And why did he go?"

"We have only one man's word for that," the conductor snarled. "I've traveled some in these cars myself, and no one ever changed berths with me."

Somebody on the edge of the group asserted that hereafter he would travel by daylight. I glanced up and caught the eye of the girl in blue.

"They are all mad," she said. Her tone was low, but I heard her distinctly. "Don't take them seriously enough to defend yourself."

"I am glad you think I didn't do it," I observed meekly, over the crowd. "Nothing else is of any importance."

The conductor had pulled out his note-book again. "Your name, please," he said gruffly.

"Lawrence Blakeley, Washington."

"Your occupation?"

"Attorney. A member of the firm of Blakeley and McKnight."

"Mr. Blakeley, you say you have occupied the wrong berth and have been robbed. Do you know anything of the man who did it?"

"Only from what he left behind," I answered. "These clothes—"

"They fit you," he said with quick suspicion. "Isn't that rather a coincidence? You are a large man."

"Good Heavens," I retorted, stung into fury, "do I look like a man who would wear this kind of a necktie? Do you suppose I carry purple and green barred silk handkerchiefs? Would any man in his senses wear a pair of shoes a full size too small?"

The conductor was inclined to hedge. "You will have to grant that I am in a peculiar position," he said. "I have only your word as to the exchange of berths, and you understand I am merely doing my duty. Are there any clues in the pockets?"

For the second time I emptied them of their contents, which he noted. "Is that all?" he finished. "There was nothing else?"

"Nothing."

"That's not all, sir," broke in the porter, stepping forward. "There was a small black satchel."

"That's so," I exclaimed. "I forgot the bag. I don't even know where it is."

The easily swayed crowd looked suspicious again. I've grown so accustomed to reading the faces of a jury, seeing them swing from doubt to belief, and back again to doubt, that I instinctively watch expressions. I saw that my forgetfulness had done me harm—that suspicion was roused again.

The bag was found a couple of seats away, under somebody's raincoat—another dubious circumstance. Was I hiding it? It was brought to the berth and placed beside the conductor, who opened it at once.

It contained the usual traveling impedimenta—change of linen, collars, handkerchiefs, a bronze-green scarf, and a safety razor. But the attention of the crowd riveted itself on a flat, Russia leather wallet, around which a heavy gum band was wrapped, and which bore in gilt letters the name "Simon Harrington."

Chapter 7

A FINE GOLD CHAIN

The conductor held it out to me, his face sternly accusing.

"Is this another coincidence?" he asked. "Did the man who left you his clothes and the barred silk handkerchief and the tight shoes leave you the spoil of the murder?"

The men standing around had drawn off a little, and I saw the absolute futility of any remonstrance. Have you ever seen a fly, who, in these hygienic days, finding no cobwebs to entangle him, is caught in a sheet of fly paper, finds himself more and more mired, and is finally quiet with the sticky stillness of despair?

Well, I was the fly. I had seen too much of circumstantial evidence to have any belief that the establishing of my identity would weigh much against the other incriminating details. It meant imprisonment and trial, probably, with all the notoriety and loss of practice they would entail. A man thinks quickly at a time like that. All the probable consequences of the finding of that pocket-book flashed through my mind as I extended my hand to take it. Then I drew my arm back.

"I don't want it," I said. "Look inside. Maybe the other man took the money and left the wallet."

The conductor opened it, and again there was a curious surging forward of the crowd. To my intense disappointment the money was still there.

I stood blankly miserable while it was counted out—five one-hundred-dollar bills, six twenties, and some fives and ones that brought the total to six hundred and fifty dollars.

The little man with the note-book insisted on taking the numbers of the notes, to the conductor's annoyance. It was immaterial to me: small things had lost their power to irritate. I was seeing myself in the prisoner's box, going through all the nerve-racking routine of a trial for murder—the challenging of the jury, the endless cross-examinations, the alternate hope and fear. I believe I said before that I had no nerves, but for a few minutes that morning I was as near as a man ever comes to hysteria.

I folded my arms and gave myself a mental shake. I seemed to be the center of a hundred eyes, expressing every shade of doubt and distrust, but I tried not to flinch. Then some one created a diversion.

The amateur detective was busy again with the seal-skin bag, investigating the make of the safety razor and the manufacturer's name on the bronze-green tie. Now, however, he paused and frowned, as though some pet theory had been upset.

Then from a corner of the bag he drew out and held up for our inspection some three inches of fine gold chain, one end of which was blackened and stained with blood!

The conductor held out his hand for it, but the little man was not ready to give it up. He turned to me.

"You say no watch was left you? Was there a piece of chain like that?"

"No chain at all," I said sulkily. "No jewelry of any kind, except plain gold buttons in the shirt I am wearing."

"Where are your glasses?" he threw at me suddenly: instinctively my hand went to my eyes. My glasses had been gone all morning, and I had not even noticed their absence. The little man smiled cynically and held out the chain.

"I must ask you to examine this," he insisted. "Isn't it a part of the fine gold chain you wear over your ear?"

I didn't want to touch the thing: the stain at the end made me shudder. But with a baker's dozen of suspicious eyes—well, we'll say fourteen: there were no one-eyed men—I took the fragment in the tips of my fingers and looked at it helplessly.

"Very fine chains are much alike," I managed to say. "For all I know, this may be mine, but I don't know how it got into that sealskin bag. I never saw the bag until this morning after daylight."

"He admits that he had the bag," somebody said behind me. "How did you guess that he wore glasses, anyhow?" to the amateur sleuth.

That gentleman cleared his throat. "There were two reasons," he said, "for suspecting it. When you see a man with the lines of his face drooping, a healthy individual with a pensive eye,—suspect astigmatism. Besides, this gentleman has a pronounced line across the bridge of his nose and a mark on his ear from the chain."

After this remarkable exhibition of the theoretical as combined with the practical, he sank into a seat near-by, and still holding the chain, sat with closed eyes and pursed lips. It was evident to all the car that the solution of the mystery was a question of moments. Once he bent forward eagerly and putting the chain on the window-sill, proceeded to go over it with a pocket magnifying glass, only to shake his head in disappointment. All the people around shook their heads too, although they had not the slightest idea what it was about.

The pounding in my ears began again. The group around me seemed to be suddenly motionless in the very act of moving, as if a hypnotist had called "Rigid!" The girl in blue was looking at me, and above the din I thought she said she must speak to me—something vital. The pounding grew louder and merged into a scream. With a grinding and splintering the car rose under my feet. Then it fell away into darkness.

Chapter 8

THE SECOND SECTION

Have you ever been picked up out of your three-meals-a-day life, whirled around in a tornado of events, and landed in a situation so grotesque and yet so horrible that you laugh even while you are groaning, and straining at its hopelessness? McKnight says that is hysteria, and that no man worthy of the name ever admits to it.

Also, as McKnight says, it sounds like a tank drama. Just as the revolving saw is about to cut the hero into stove lengths, the second villain blows up the sawmill. The hero goes up through the roof and alights on the bank of a stream at the feet of his lady love, who is making daisy chains.

Nevertheless, when I was safely home again, with Mrs. Klopton brewing strange drinks that came in paper packets from the pharmacy, and that smelled to heaven, I remember staggering to the door and closing it, and then going back to bed and howling out the absurdity and the madness of the whole thing. And while I laughed my very soul was sick, for the girl was gone by that time, and I knew by all the loyalty that answers between men for honor that I would have to put her out of my mind.

And yet, all the night that followed, filled as it was with the shrieking demons of pain, I saw her as I had seen her last, in the queer hat with green ribbons. I told the doctor this, guardedly, the next morning, and he said it was the morphia, and that I was lucky not to have seen a row of devils with green tails.

I don't know anything about the wreck of September ninth last. You who swallowed the details with your coffee and digested the horrors with your chop, probably know a great deal more than I do. I remember very distinctly that the jumping and throbbing in my arm brought me back to a world that at first was nothing but sky, a heap of clouds that I thought hazily were the meringue on a blue charlotte russe. As the sense of hearing was slowly added to vision, I heard a woman near me sobbing that she had lost her hat pin, and she couldn't keep her hat on.

I think I dropped back into unconsciousness again, for the next thing I remember was of my blue patch of sky clouded with smoke, of a strange roaring and crackling, of a rain of fiery sparks on my face and of somebody beating at me with feeble hands. I opened my eyes and closed them again: the girl in blue was bending over me. With that imperviousness to big things and keenness to small that is the first effect of shock, I tried to be facetious, when a spark stung my cheek.

"You will have to rouse yourself!" the girl was repeating desperately. "You've been on fire twice already." A piece of striped ticking floated slowly over my head. As the wind caught it its charring edges leaped into flame.

"Looks like a kite, doesn't it?" I remarked cheerfully. And then, as my arm gave an excruciating throb— "Jove, how my arm hurts!"

The girl bent over and spoke slowly, distinctly, as one might speak to a deaf person or a child.

"Listen, Mr. Blakeley," she said earnestly. "You must rouse yourself. There has been a terrible accident. The second section ran into us. The wreck is burning now, and if we don't move, we will catch fire. Do you hear?"

Her voice and my arm were bringing me to my senses. "I hear," I said. "I—I'll sit up in a second. Are you hurt?"

"No, only bruised. Do you think you can walk?"

I drew up one foot after another, gingerly.

"They seem to move all right," I remarked dubiously. "Would you mind telling me where the back of my head has gone? I can't help thinking it isn't there."

She made a quick examination. "It's pretty badly bumped," she said. "You must have fallen on it."

I had got up on my uninjured elbow by that time, but the pain threw me back. "Don't look at the wreck," I entreated her. "It's no sight for a woman. If—if there is any way to tie up this arm, I might be able to do something. There may be people under those cars!"

"Then it is too late to help," she replied solemnly. A little shower of feathers, each carrying its fiery lamp, blew over us from some burning pillow. A part the wreck collapsed with a crash. In a resolute to play a man's part in the tragedy going on around, I got to my knees. Then I realized what had not noticed before: the hand and wrist of the broken left arm were jammed through the handle of the sealskin grip. I gasped and sat down suddenly.

"You must not do that," the girl insisted. I noticed now that she kept her back to the wreck, her eyes averted. "The weight of the traveling-bag must be agony. Let me support the valise until we get back a few yards. Then you must lie down until we can get it cut off."

"Will it have to be cut off?" I asked as calmly as possible. There were red-hot stabs of agony clear to my neck, but we were moving slowly away from the track.

"Yes," she replied, with dumfounding coolness. "If I had a knife I could do it myself. You might sit here and lean against this fence."

By that time my returning faculties had realized that she was going to cut off the satchel, not the arm. The dizziness was leaving and I was gradually becoming myself.

"If you pull, it might come," I suggested. "And with that weight gone, I think I will cease to be five feet eleven inches of baby."

She tried gently to loosen the handle, but it would not move, and at last, with great drops of cold perspiration over me, I had to give up.

"I'm afraid I can't stand it," I said. "But there's a knife somewhere around these clothes, and if I can find it, perhaps you can cut the leather."

As I gave her the knife she turned it over, examining it with a peculiar expression, bewilderment rather than surprise. But she said nothing. She set to work deftly, and in a few minutes the bag dropped free.

"That's better," I declared, sitting up. "Now, if you can pin my sleeve to my coat, it will support the arm so we can get away from here."

"The pin might give," she objected, "and the jerk would be terrible." She looked around, puzzled; then she got up, coming back in a minute with a draggled, partly scorched sheet. This she tore into a large square, and after she had folded it, she slipped it under the broken arm and tied it securely at the back of my neck.

The relief was immediate, and, picking up the sealskin bag, I walked slowly beside her, away from the track.

The first act was over: the curtain fallen. The scene was "struck."

Chapter 9

THE HALCYON BREAKFAST

We were still dazed, I think, for we wandered like two troubled children, our one idea at first to get as far away as we could from the horror behind us. We were both bareheaded, grimy, pallid through the grit. Now and then we met little groups of country folk hurrying to the track: they stared at us curiously, and some wished to question us. But we hurried past them; we had put the wreck behind us. That way lay madness.

Only once the girl turned and looked behind her. The wreck was hidden, but the smoke cloud hung heavy and dense. For the first time I remembered that my companion had not been alone on the train.

"It is quiet here," I suggested. "If you will sit down on the bank I will go back and make some inquiries. I've been criminally thoughtless. Your traveling companion—"

She interrupted me, and something of her splendid poise was gone. "Please don't go back," she said. "I am afraid it would be of no use. And I don't want to be left alone."

Heaven knows I did not want her to be alone. I was more than content to walk along beside her aimlessly, for any length of time. Gradually, as she lost the exaltation of the moment, I was gaining my normal condition of mind. I was beginning to realize that I had lacked the morning grace of a shave, that I looked like some lost hope of yesterday, and that my left shoe pinched outrageously. A man does not rise triumphant above such handicaps. The girl, for all her disordered hair and the crumpled linen of her waist, in spite of her missing hat and the small gold bag that hung forlornly from a broken chain, looked exceedingly lovely.

"Then I won't leave you alone," I said manfully, and we stumbled on together. Thus far we had seen nobody from the wreck, but well up the lane we came across the tall dark woman who had occupied lower eleven. She was half crouching beside the road, her black hair about her shoulders, and an ugly bruise over her eye. She did not seem to know us, and refused to accompany us. We left her there at last, babbling incoherently and rolling in her hands a dozen pebbles she had gathered in the road.

The girl shuddered as we went on. Once she turned and glanced at my bandage. "Does it hurt very much?" she asked.

"It's growing rather numb. But it might be worse," I answered mendaciously. If anything in this world could be worse, I had never experienced it.

And so we trudged on bareheaded under the summer sun, growing parched and dusty and weary, doggedly leaving behind us the pillar of smoke. I thought I knew of a trolley line somewhere in the direction we were going, or perhaps we could find a horse and trap to take us into Baltimore. The girl smiled when I suggested it.

"We will create a sensation, won't we?" she asked. "Isn't it queer—or perhaps it's my state of mind—but I keep wishing for a pair of gloves, when I haven't even a hat!"

When we reached the main road we sat down for a moment, and her hair, which had been coming loose for some time, fell over her shoulders in little waves that were most alluring. It seemed a pity to twist it up again, but when I suggested this, cautiously, she said it was troublesome and got in her eyes when it was loose. So she gathered it up, while I held a row of little shell combs and pins, and when it was done it was vastly becoming, too. Funny about hair: a man never knows he has it until he begins to lose it, but it's different with a girl. Something of the unconventional situation began to dawn on her as she put in the last hair-pin and patted some stray locks to place.

"I have not told you my name," she said abruptly. "I forgot that because I know who you are, you know nothing about me. I am Alison West, and my home is in Richmond."

So that was it! This was the girl of the photograph on John Gilmore's bedside table. The girl McKnight expected to see in Richmond the next day, Sunday! She was on her way back to meet him! Well, what difference did it make, anyhow? We had been thrown together by the merest chance. In an hour or two at the most we would be back in civilization and she would recall me, if she remembered me at all, as an unshaven creature in a red cravat and tan shoes, with a soiled Pullman sheet tied around my neck. I drew a deep breath.

"Just a twinge," I said, when she glanced up quickly. "It's very good of you to let me know, Miss West. I have been hearing delightful things about you for three months."

"From Richey McKnight?" She was frankly curious.

"Yes. From Richey McKnight," I assented. Was it any wonder McKnight was crazy about her? I dug my heels into the dust.

"I have been visiting near Cresson, in the mountains," Miss West was saying. "The person you mentioned, Mrs. Curtis, was my hostess. We—we were on our way to Washington together." She spoke slowly, as if she wished to give the minimum of explanation. Across her face had come again the baffling expression of perplexity and trouble I had seen before.

"You were on your way home, I suppose? Richey spoke about seeing you," I floundered, finding it necessary to say something. She looked at me with level, direct eyes.

"No," she returned quietly. "I did not intend to go home. I—well, it doesn't matter; I am going home now."

A woman in a calico dress, with two children, each an exact duplicate of the other, had come quickly down the road. She took in the situation at a glance, and was explosively hospitable.

"You poor things," she said. "If you'll take the first road to the left over there, and turn in at the second pigsty, you will find breakfast on the table and a coffee-pot on the stove. And there's plenty of soap and water, too. Don't say one word. There isn't a soul there to see you."

We accepted the invitation and she hurried on toward the excitement and the railroad. I got up carefully and helped Miss West to her feet.

"At the second pigsty to the left," I repeated, "we will find the breakfast I promised you seven eternities ago. Forward to the pigsty!"

We said very little for the remainder of that walk. I had almost reached the limit of endurance: with every step the broken ends of the bone grated together. We found the farm-house without difficulty, and I remember wondering if I could hold out to the end of the old stone walk that led between hedges to the door.

"Allah be praised," I said with all the voice I could muster. "Behold the coffee-pot!" And then I put down the grip and folded up like a jack-knife on the porch floor.

When I came around something hot was trickling down my neck, and a despairing voice was saying, "Oh, I don't seem to be able to pour it into your mouth. Please open your eyes."

"But I don't want it in my eyes," I replied dreamily. "I haven't any idea what came over me. It was the shoes, I think: the left one is a red-hot torture." I was sitting by that time and looking across into her face.

Never before or since have I fainted, but I would do it joyfully, a dozen times a day, if I could waken again to the blissful touch of soft fingers on my face, the hot ecstasy of coffee spilled by those fingers down my neck. There was a thrill in every tone of her voice that morning. Before long my loyalty to McKnight would step between me and the girl he loved: life would develop new complexities. In those early hours after the wreck, full of pain as they were, there was nothing of the suspicion and distrust that came later. Shorn of our gauds and baubles, we were primitive man and woman, together: our world for the hour was the deserted farm-house, the slope of wheat-field that led to the road, the woodland lot, the pasture.

We breakfasted together across the homely table. Our cheerfulness, at first sheer reaction, became less forced as we ate great slices of bread from the granny oven back of the house, and drank hot fluid that smelled like coffee and tasted like nothing that I have ever swallowed. We found cream in stone jars, sunk deep in the chill water of the spring house. And there were eggs, great yellow-brown ones,—a basket of them.

So, like two children awakened from a nightmare, we chattered over our food: we hunted mutual friends, we laughed together at my feeble witticisms, but we put the horror behind us resolutely. After all, it was the hat with the green ribbons that brought back the strangeness of the situation.

All along I had had the impression that Alison West was deliberately putting out of her mind something that obtruded now and then. It brought with it a return of the puzzled expression that I had surprised early in the day, before the wreck. I caught it once, when, breakfast over, she was tightening the sling that held the broken arm. I had prolonged the morning meal as much as I could, but when the wooden clock with the pink roses on the dial pointed to half after ten, and the mother with the duplicate youngsters had not come back, Miss West made the move I had dreaded.

"If we are to get into Baltimore at all we must start," she said, rising. "You ought to see a doctor as soon as possible."

"Hush," I said warningly. "Don't mention the arm, please; it is asleep now. You may rouse it."

"If I only had a hat," she reflected. "It wouldn't need to be much of one, but—" She gave a little cry and darted to the corner. "Look," she said triumphantly, "the very thing. With the green streamers tied up in a bow, like this—do you suppose the child would mind? I can put five dollars or so here—that would buy a dozen of them."

It was a queer affair of straw, that hat, with a round crown and a rim that flopped dismally. With a single movement she had turned it up at one side and fitted it to her head. Grotesque by itself, when she wore it it was a thing of joy.

Evidently the lack of head covering had troubled her, for she was elated at her find. She left me, scrawling a note of thanks and pinning it with a bill to the table-cloth, and ran up-stairs to the mirror and the promised soap and water.

I did not see her when she came down. I had discovered a bench with a tin basin outside the kitchen door, and was washing, in a helpless, one-sided way. I felt rather than saw that she was standing in the door-way, and I made a final plunge into the basin.

"How is it possible for a man with only a right hand to wash his left ear?" I asked from the roller towel. I was distinctly uncomfortable: men are more rigidly creatures of convention than women, whether they admit it or not. "There is so much soap on me still that if I laugh I will blow bubbles. Washing with rain-water and home-made soap is like motoring on a slippery road. I only struck the high places."

Then, having achieved a brilliant polish with the towel, I looked at the girl.

She was leaning against the frame of the door, her face perfectly colorless, her breath coming in slow, difficult respirations. The erratic hat was pinned to place, but it had slid rakishly to one side. When I realized that she was staring, not at me, but past me to the road along which we had come, I turned and followed her gaze. There was no one in sight: the lane stretched dust white in the sun,—no moving figure on it, no sign of life.

Chapter 10

MISS WEST'S REQUEST

The surprising change in her held me speechless. All the animation of the breakfast table was gone: there was no hint of the response with which, before, she had met my nonsensical sallies. She stood there, white-lipped, unsmiling, staring down the dusty road. One hand was clenched tight over some small object. Her eyes dropped to it from the distant road, and then closed, with a quick, indrawn breath. Her color came back slowly. Whatever had caused the change, she said nothing. She was anxious to leave at once, almost impatient over my deliberate masculine way of getting my things together. Afterward I recalled that I had wanted to explore the barn for a horse and some sort of a vehicle to take us to the trolley, and that she had refused to allow me to look. I remembered many things later that might have helped me, and did not. At the time, I was only completely bewildered. Save the wreck, the responsibility for which lay between Providence and the engineer of the second section, all the events of that strange morning were logically connected; they came from one cause, and tended unerringly to one end. But the cause was buried, the end not yet in view.

Not until we had left the house well behind did the girl's face relax its tense lines. I was watching her more closely than I had realized, for when we had gone a little way along the road she turned to me almost petulantly. "Please don't stare so at me," she said, to my sudden confusion. "I know the hat is dreadful. Green always makes me look ghastly."

"Perhaps it was the green." I was unaccountably relieved. "Do you know, a few minutes ago, you looked almost pallid to me!"

She glanced at me quickly, but I was gazing ahead. We were out of sight of the house, now, and with every step away from it the girl was obviously relieved. Whatever she held in her hand, she never glanced at it. But she was conscious of it every second. She seemed to come to a decision about it while we were still in sight of the gate, for she murmured something and turned back alone, going swiftly, her feet stirring up small puffs of dust at every step. She fastened something to the gate-post,—I could see the nervous haste with which she worked. When she joined me again it was without explanation. But the clenched fingers were free now, and while she looked tired and worn, the strain had visibly relaxed.

We walked along slowly in the general direction of the suburban trolley line. Once a man with an empty wagon offered us a lift, but after a glance at the springless vehicle I declined.

"The ends of the bone think they are castanets as it is," I explained. "But the lady—"

The young lady, however, declined and we went on together. Once, when the trolley line was in sight, she got a pebble in her low shoe, and we sat down under a tree until she found the cause of the trouble.

"I—I don't know what I should have done without you," I blundered. "Moral support and—and all that. Do you know, my first conscious thought after the wreck was of relief that you had not been hurt?"

She was sitting beside me, where a big chestnut tree shaded the road, and I surprised a look of misery on her face that certainly my words had not been meant to produce.

"And my first thought," she said slowly, "was regret that I—that I hadn't been obliterated, blown out like a candle. Please don't look like that! I am only talking."

But her lips were trembling, and because the little shams of society are forgotten at times like this, I leaned over and patted her hand lightly, where it rested on the grass beside me.

"You must not say those things," I expostulated. "Perhaps, after all, your friends—"

"I had no friends on the train." Her voice was hard again, her tone final. She drew her hand from under mine, not quickly, but decisively. A car was in sight, coming toward us. The steel finger of civilization, of propriety, of visiting cards and formal introductions was beckoning us in. Miss West put on her shoe.

We said little on the car. The few passengers stared at us frankly, and discussed the wreck, emphasizing its horrors. The girl did not seem to hear. Once she turned to me with the quick, unexpected movement that was one of her charms.

"I do not wish my mother to know I was in the accident," she said. "Will you please not tell Richey about having met me?"

I gave my promise, of course. Again, when we were almost into Baltimore, she asked to examine the gun-metal cigarette case, and sat silent with it in her hands, while I told of the early morning's events on the Ontario.

"So you see," I finished, "this grip, everything I have on, belongs to a fellow named Sullivan. He probably left the train before the wreck,—perhaps just after the murder."

"And so—you think he committed the—the crime?" Her eyes were on the cigarette case.

"Naturally," I said. "A man doesn't jump off a Pullman car in the middle of the night in another man's clothes, unless he is trying to get away from something. Besides the dirk, there were the stains that you, saw. Why, I have the murdered man's pocket-book in this valise at my feet. What does that look like?"

I colored when I saw the ghost of a smile hovering around the corners of her mouth. "That is," I finished, "if you care to believe that I am innocent."

The sustaining chain of her small gold bag gave way just then. She did not notice it. I picked it up and slid the trinket into my pocket for safekeeping, where I promptly forgot it. Afterwards I wished I had let it lie unnoticed on the floor of that dirty little suburban car, and even now, when I see a woman carelessly dangling a similar feminine trinket, I shudder involuntarily: there comes back to me the memory of a girl's puzzled eyes under the brim of a flopping hat, the haunting suspicion of the sleepless nights that followed.

Just then I was determined that my companion should not stray back to the wreck, and to that end I was determinedly facetious.

"Do you know that it is Sunday?" she asked suddenly, "and that we are actually ragged?"

"Never mind that," I retorted. "All Baltimore is divided on Sunday into three parts, those who rise up and go to church, those who rise up and read the newspapers, and those who don't rise up. The first are somewhere between the creed and the sermon, and we need not worry about the others."

"You treat me like a child," she said almost pettishly. "Don't try so hard to be cheerful. It—it is almost ghastly."

After that I subsided like a pricked balloon, and the remainder of the ride was made in silence. The information that she would go to friends in the city was a shock: it meant an earlier separation than I had planned for. But my arm was beginning again. In putting her into a cab I struck it and gritted my teeth with the pain. It was probably for that reason that I forgot the gold bag.

She leaned forward and held out her hand. "I may not have another chance to thank you," she said, "and I think I would better not try, anyhow. I cannot tell you how grateful I am." I muttered something about the gratitude being mine: owing to the knock I was seeing two cabs, and two girls were holding out two hands.

"Remember," they were both saying, "you have never met me, Mr. Blakeley. And—if you ever hear anything about me—that is not—pleasant, I want you to think the best you can of me. Will you?"

The two girls were one now, with little flashes of white light playing all around. "I—I'm afraid that I shall think too well for my own good," I said unsteadily. And the cab drove on.

Chapter 11

THE NAME WAS SULLIVAN

I had my arm done up temporarily in Baltimore and took the next train home. I was pretty far gone when I stumbled out of a cab almost into the scandalized arms of Mrs. Klopton. In fifteen minutes I was in bed, with that good woman piling on blankets and blistering me in unprotected places with hot-water bottles. And in an hour I had a whiff of chloroform and Doctor Williams had set the broken bone.

I dropped asleep then, waking in the late twilight to a realization that I was at home again, without the papers that meant conviction for Andy Bronson, with a charge of murder hanging over my head, and with something more than an impression of the girl my best friend was in love with, a girl moreover who was almost as great an enigma as the crime itself.

"And I'm no hand at guessing riddles," I groaned half aloud. Mrs. Klopton came over promptly and put a cold cloth on my forehead.

"Euphemia," she said to some one outside the door, "telephone the doctor that he is still rambling, but that he has switched from green ribbons to riddles."

"There's nothing the matter with me, Mrs. Klopton," I rebelled. "I was only thinking out loud. Confound that cloth: it's trickling all over me!" I gave it a fling, and heard it land with a soggy thud on the floor.

"Thinking out loud is delirium," Mrs. Klopton said imperturbably. "A fresh cloth, Euphemia."

This time she held it on with a firm pressure that I was too weak to resist. I expostulated feebly that I was drowning, which she also laid to my mental exaltation, and then I finally dropped into a damp sleep. It was probably midnight when I roused again. I had been dreaming of the wreck, and it was inexpressibly comforting to feel the stability of my bed, and to realize the equal stability of Mrs. Klopton, who sat, fully attired, by the night light, reading Science and Health.

"Does that book say anything about opening the windows on a hot night?" I suggested, when I had got my bearings.

She put it down immediately and came over to me. If there is one time when Mrs. Klopton is chastened— and it is the only time—it is when she reads Science and Health. "I don't like to open the shutters, Mr. Lawrence," she explained. "Not since the night you went away."

But, pressed further, she refused to explain. "The doctor said you were not to be excited," she persisted. "Here's your beef tea."

"Not a drop until you tell me," I said firmly. "Besides, you know very well there's nothing the matter with me. This arm of mine is only a false belief." I sat up gingerly. "Now—why don't you open that window?"

Mrs. Klopton succumbed. "Because there are queer goings-on in that house next door," she said. "If you will take the beef tea, Mr. Lawrence, I will tell you."

The queer goings-on, however, proved to be slightly disappointing. It seemed that after I left on Friday night, a light was seen flitting fitfully through the empty house next door. Euphemia had seen it first and called Mrs. Klopton. Together they had watched it breathlessly until it disappeared on the lower floor.

"You should have been a writer of ghost stories," I said, giving my pillows a thump. "And so it was fitting flitfully!"

"That's what it was doing," she reiterated. "Fitting flitfully—I mean flitting fitfully—how you do throw me out, Mr. Lawrence! And what's more, it came again!"

"Oh, come now, Mrs. Klopton," I objected, "ghosts are like lightning; they never strike twice in the same night. That is only worth half a cup of beef tea."

"You may ask Euphemia," she retorted with dignity. "Not more than an hour after, there was a light there again. We saw it through the chinks of the shutters. Only—this time it began at the lower floor and climbed!"

"You oughtn't to tell ghost stories at night," came McKnight's voice from the doorway. "Really, Mrs. Klopton, I'm amazed at you. You old duffer! I've got you to thank for the worst day of my life."

Mrs. Klopton gulped. Then realizing that the "old duffer" was meant for me, she took her empty cup and went out muttering.

"The Pirate's crazy about me, isn't she?" McKnight said to the closing door. Then he swung around and held out his hand.

"By Jove," he said, "I've been laying you out all day, lilies on the door-bell, black gloves, everything. If you had had the sense of a mosquito in a snow-storm, you would have telephoned me."

"I never even thought of it." I was filled with remorse. "Upon my word, Rich, I hadn't an idea beyond getting away from that place. If you had seen what I saw—"

McKnight stopped me. "Seen it! Why, you lunatic, I've been digging for you all day in the ruins! I've lunched and dined on horrors. Give me something to rinse them down, Lollie."

He had fished the key of the cellarette from its hiding-place in my shoe bag and was mixing himself what he called a Bernard Shaw—a foundation of brandy and soda, with a little of everything else in sight to give it snap. Now that I saw him clearly, he looked weary and grimy. I hated to tell him what I knew he was waiting to hear, but there was no use wading in by inches. I ducked and got it over.

"The notes are gone, Rich," I said, as quietly as I could. In spite of himself his face fell.

"I—of course I expected it," he said. "But—Mrs. Klopton said over the telephone that you had brought home a grip and I hoped—well, Lord knows we ought not to complain. You're here, damaged, but here." He lifted his glass. "Happy days, old man!"

"If you will give me that black bottle and a teaspoon, I'll drink that in arnica, or whatever the stuff is; Rich,—the notes were gone before the wreck!"

He wheeled and stared at me, the bottle in his hand. "Lost, strayed or stolen?" he queried with forced lightness.

"Stolen, although I believe the theft was incidental to something else."

Mrs. Klopton came in at that moment, with an eggnog in her hand. She glanced at the clock, and, without addressing any one in particular, she intimated that it was time for self-respecting folks to be at home in bed. McKnight, who could never resist a fling at her back, spoke to me in a stage whisper.

"Is she talking still? or again?" he asked, just before the door closed. There was a second's indecision with the knob, then, judging discretion the better part, Mrs. Klopton went away.

"Now, then," McKnight said, settling himself in a chair beside the bed, "spit it out. Not the wreck—I know all I want about that. But the theft. I can tell you beforehand that it was a woman."

I had crawled painfully out of bed, and was in the act of pouring the egg-nog down the pipe of the washstand. I paused, with the glass in the air.

"A woman!" I repeated, startled. "What makes you think that?"

"You don't know the first principles of a good detective yarn," he said scornfully. "Of course, it was the woman in the empty house next door. You said it was brass pipes, you will remember. Well—on with the dance: let joy be unconfined."

So I told the story; I had told it so many times that day that I did it automatically. And I told about the girl with the bronze hair, and my suspicions. But I did not mention Alison West. McKnight listened to the end without interruption. When I had finished he drew a long breath.

"Well!" he said. "That's something of a mess, isn't it? If you can only prove your mild and child-like disposition, they couldn't hold you for the murder—which is a regular ten-twent-thirt crime, anyhow. But the notes—that's different. They are not burned, anyhow. Your man wasn't on the train—therefore, he wasn't in the wreck. If he didn't know what he was taking, as you seem to think, he probably reads the papers, and unless he is a fathead, he's awake by this time to what he's got. He'll try to sell them to Bronson, probably."

"Or to us," I put in.

We said nothing for a few minutes. McKnight smoked a cigarette and stared at a photograph of Candida over the mantel. Candida is the best pony for a heavy mount in seven states.

"I didn't go to Richmond," he observed finally. The remark followed my own thoughts so closely that I started. "Miss West is not home yet from Seal Harbor."

Receiving no response, he lapsed again into thoughtful silence. Mrs. Klopton came in just as the clock struck one, and made preparation for the night by putting a large gaudy comfortable into an arm-chair in the dressing-room, with a smaller, stiff-backed chair for her feet. She was wonderfully attired in a dressing-gown that was reminiscent, in parts, of all the ones she had given me for a half dozen Christmases, and she had a purple veil wrapped around her head, to hide Heaven knows what deficiency. She examined the empty egg-nog glass, inquired what the evening paper had said about the weather, and then stalked into the dressing-room, and prepared, with much ostentatious creaking, to sit up all night.

We fell silent again, while McKnight traced a rough outline of the berths on the white table-cover, and puzzled it out slowly. It was something like this:

```
 _____
| 12 | 10 | 8 |

|_____|

|___AISLE____|

| 11 | 9 | 7 |

|_____|
```

"You think he changed the tags on seven and nine, so that when you went back to bed you thought you were crawling into nine, when it was really seven, eh?"

"Probably—yes."

"Then toward morning, when everybody was asleep, your theory is that he changed the numbers again and left the train."

"I can't think of anything else," I replied wearily.

"Jove, what a game of bridge that fellow would play! It was like finessing an eight-spot and winning out. They would scarcely have doubted your story had the tags been reversed in the morning. He certainly left you in a bad way. Not a jury in the country would stand out against the stains, the stiletto, and the murdered man's pocket-book in your possession."

"Then you think Sullivan did it?" I asked.

"Of course," said McKnight confidently. "Unless you did it in your sleep. Look at the stains on his pillow, and the dirk stuck into it. And didn't he have the man Harrington's pocket-book?"

"But why did he go off without the money?" I persisted. "And where does the bronze-haired girl come in?"

"Search me," McKnight retorted flippantly. "Inflammation of the imagination on your part."

"Then there is the piece of telegram. It said lower ten, car seven. It's extremely likely that she had it. That telegram was about me, Richey."

"I'm getting a headache," he said, putting out his cigarette against the sole of his shoe. "All I'm certain of just now is that if there hadn't been a wreck, by this time you'd be sitting in an eight by ten cell, and feeling like the rhyme for it."

"But listen to this," I contended, as he picked up his hat, "this fellow Sullivan is a fugitive, and he's a lot more likely to make advances to Bronson than to us. We could have the case continued, release Bronson on bail and set a watch on him."

"Not my watch," McKnight protested. "It's a family heirloom."

"You'd better go home," I said firmly. "Go home and go to bed. You're sleepy. You can have Sullivan's red necktie to dream over if you think it will help any."

Mrs. Klopton's voice came drowsily from the next room, punctuated by a yawn. "Oh, I forgot to tell you," she called, with the suspicious lisp which characterizes her at night, "somebody called up about noon, Mr. Lawrence. It was long distance, and he said he would call again. The name was"—she yawned—"Sullivan."

Chapter 12

THE GOLD BAG

I have always smiled at those cases of spontaneous combustion which, like fusing the component parts of a seidlitz powder, unite two people in a bubbling and ephemeral ecstasy. But surely there is possible, with but a single meeting, an attraction so great, a community of mind and interest so strong, that between that first meeting and the next the bond may grow into something stronger. This is especially true, I fancy, of people with temperament, the modern substitute for imagination. It is a nice question whether lovers begin to love when they are together, or when they are apart.

Not that I followed any such line of reasoning at the time. I would not even admit my folly to myself. But during the restless hours of that first night after the accident, when my back ached with lying on it, and any other position was torture, I found my thoughts constantly going back to Alison West. I dropped into a doze, to dream of touching her fingers again to comfort her, and awoke to find I had patted a teaspoonful of medicine out of Mrs. Klopton's indignant hand. What was it McKnight had said about making an egregious ass of myself?

And that brought me back to Richey, and I fancy I groaned. There is no use expatiating on the friendship between two men who have gone together through college, have quarreled and made it up, fussed together over politics and debated creeds for years: men don't need to be told, and women can not understand. Nevertheless, I groaned. If it had been any one but Rich!

Some things were mine, however, and I would hold them: the halcyon breakfast, the queer hat, the pebble in her small shoe, the gold bag with the broken chain—the bag! Why, it was in my pocket at that moment.

I got up painfully and found my coat. Yes, there was the purse, bulging with an opulent suggestion of wealth inside. I went back to bed again, somewhat dizzy, between effort and the touch of the trinket, so lately hers. I held it up by its broken chain and gloated over it. By careful attention to orders, I ought to be out in a day or so. Then—I could return it to her. I really ought to do that: it was valuable, and I wouldn't care to trust it to the mail. I could run down to Richmond, and see her once—there was no disloyalty to Rich in that.

I had no intention of opening the little bag. I put it under my pillow—which was my reason for refusing to have the linen slips changed, to Mrs. Klopton's dismay. And sometimes during the morning, while I lay under a virgin field of white, ornamented with strange flowers, my cigarettes hidden beyond discovery, and Science and Health on a table by my elbow, as if by the merest accident, I slid my hand under my pillow and touched it reverently.

McKnight came in about eleven. I heard his car at the curb, followed almost immediately by his slam at the front door, and his usual clamor on the stairs. He had a bottle under his arm, rightly surmising that I had been forbidden stimulant, and a large box of cigarettes in his pocket, suspecting my deprivation.

"Well," he said cheerfully. "How did you sleep after keeping me up half the night?"

I slid my hand around: the purse was well covered. "Have it now, or wait till I get the cork out?" he rattled on.

"I don't want anything," I protested. "I wish you wouldn't be so darned cheerful, Richey." He stopped whistling to stare at me.

"'I am saddest when I sing!'" he quoted unctuously. "It's pure reaction, Lollie. Yesterday the sky was low: I was digging for my best friend. To-day—he lies before me, his peevish self. Yesterday I thought the notes were burned: to-day—I look forward to a good cross-country chase, and with luck we will draw." His voice changed suddenly. "Yesterday—she was in Seal Harbor. To-day—she is here."

"Here in Washington?" I asked, as naturally as I could.

"Yes. Going to stay a week or two."

"Oh, I had a little hen and she had a wooden leg

And nearly every morning she used to lay an egg—"

"Will you stop that racket, Rich! It's the real thing this time, I suppose?"

"She's the best little chicken that we have on the farm

And another little drink won't do us any harm—"

he finished, twisting out the corkscrew. Then he came over and sat down on the bed.

"Well," he said judicially, "since you drag it from me, I think perhaps it is. You—you're such a confirmed woman-hater that I hardly knew how you would take it."

"Nothing of the sort," I denied testily. "Because a man reaches the age of thirty without making maudlin love to every—"

"I've taken to long country rides," he went on reflectively, without listening to me, "and yesterday I ran over a sheep; nearly went into the ditch. But there's a Providence that watches over fools and lovers, and just now I know darned well that I'm one, and I have a sneaking idea I'm both."

"You are both," I said with disgust. "If you can be rational for one moment, I wish you would tell me why that man Sullivan called me over the telephone yesterday morning."

"Probably hadn't yet discovered the Bronson notes—providing you hold to your theory that the theft was incidental to the murder. May have wanted his own clothes again, or to thank you for yours. Search me: I can't think of anything else." The doctor came in just then.

As I said before, I think a lot of my doctor—when I am ill. He is a young man, with an air of breezy self-confidence and good humor. He looked directly past the bottle, which is a very valuable accomplishment, and shook hands with McKnight until I could put the cigarettes under the bedclothes. He had interdicted tobacco. Then he sat down beside the bed and felt around the bandages with hands as gentle as a baby's.

"Pretty good shape," he said. "How did you sleep?"

"Oh, occasionally," I replied. "I would like to sit up, doctor."

"Nonsense. Take a rest while you have an excuse for it. I wish to thunder I could stay in bed for a day or so. I was up all night."

"Have a drink," McKnight said, pushing over the bottle.

"Twins!" The doctor grinned.

"Have two drinks."

But the medical man refused.

"I wouldn't even wear a champagne-colored necktie during business hours," he explained. "By the way, I had another case from your accident, Mr. Blakeley, late yesterday afternoon. Under the tongue, please." He stuck a thermometer in my mouth.

I had a sudden terrible vision of the amateur detective coming to light, note-book, cheerful impertinence and incriminating data. "A small man?" I demanded, "gray hair—"

"Keep your mouth closed," the doctor said peremptorily. "No. A woman, with a fractured skull. Beautiful case. Van Kirk was up to his eyes and sent for me. Hemorrhage, right-sided paralysis, irregular pupils—all the trimmings. Worked for two hours."

"Did she recover?" McKnight put in. He was examining the doctor with a new awe.

"She lifted her right arm before I left," the doctor finished cheerily, "so the operation was a success, even if she should die."

"Good Heavens," McKnight broke in, "and I thought you were just an ordinary mortal, like the rest of us! Let me touch you for luck. Was she pretty?"

"Yes, and young. Had a wealth of bronze-colored hair. Upon my soul, I hated to cut it."

McKnight and I exchanged glances.

"Do you know her name, doctor?" I asked.

"No. The nurses said her clothes came from a Pittsburg tailor."

"She is not conscious, I suppose?"

"No; she may be, to-morrow—or in a week."

He looked at the thermometer, murmured something about liquid diet, avoiding my eye—Mrs. Klopton was broiling a chop at the time—and took his departure, humming cheerfully as he went down-stairs. McKnight looked after him wistfully.

"Jove, I wish I had his constitution," he exclaimed. "Neither nerves nor heart! What a chauffeur he would make!"

But I was serious.

"I have an idea," I said grimly, "that this small matter of the murder is going to come up again, and that your uncle will be in the deuce of a fix if it does. If that woman is going to die, somebody ought to be around to take her deposition. She knows a lot, if she didn't do it herself. I wish you would go down to the telephone and get the hospital. Find out her name, and if she is conscious."

McKnight went under protest. "I haven't much time," he said, looking at his watch. "I'm to meet Mrs. West and Alison at one. I want you to know them, Lollie. You would like the mother."

"Why not the daughter?" I inquired. I touched the little gold bag under the pillow.

"Well," he said judicially, "you've always declared against the immaturity and romantic nonsense of very young women—"

"I never said anything of the sort," I retorted furiously.

"'There is more satisfaction to be had out of a good saddle horse!'" he quoted me. "'More excitement out of a polo pony, and as for the eternal matrimonial chase, give me instead a good stubble, a fox, some decent hounds and a hunter, and I'll show you the real joys of the chase!'"

"For Heaven's sake, go down to the telephone, you make my head ache," I said savagely.

I hardly know what prompted me to take out the gold purse and look at it. It was an imbecile thing to do—call it impulse, sentimentality, what you wish. I brought it out, one eye on the door, for Mrs. Klopton has a ready eye and a noiseless shoe. But the house was quiet. Down-stairs McKnight was flirting with the telephone central and there was an odor of boneset tea in the air. I think Mrs. Klopton was fascinated out of her theories by the "boneset" in connection with the fractured arm.

Anyhow, I held up the bag and looked at it. It must have been unfastened, for the next instant there was an avalanche on the snowfield of the counterpane—some money, a wisp of a handkerchief, a tiny booklet with thin leaves, covered with a powdery substance—and a necklace. I drew myself up slowly and stared at the necklace.

It was one of the semi-barbaric affairs that women are wearing now, a heavy pendant of gold chains and carved cameos, swung from a thin neck chain of the same metal. The necklace was broken: in three places the links were pulled apart and the cameos swung loose and partly detached. But it was the supporting chain that held my eye and fascinated with its sinister suggestion. Three inches of it had been snapped off, and as well as I knew anything on earth, I knew that the bit of chain that the amateur detective had found, blood-stain and all, belonged just there.

And there was no one I could talk to about it, no one to tell me how hideously absurd it was, no one to give me a slap and tell me there are tons of fine gold chains made every year, or to point out the long arm of coincidence!

With my one useful hand I fumbled the things back into the bag and thrust it deep out of sight among the pillows. Then I lay back in a cold perspiration. What connection had Alison West with this crime? Why had she stared so at the gun-metal cigarette case that morning on the train? What had alarmed her so at the farm-house? What had she taken back to the gate? Why did she wish she had not escaped from the wreck? And last, in Heaven's name, how did a part of her necklace become torn off and covered with blood?

Down-stairs McKnight was still at the telephone, and amusing himself with Mrs. Klopton in the interval of waiting.

"Why did he come home in a gray suit, when he went away in a blue?" he repeated. "Well, wrecks are queer things, Mrs. Klopton. The suit may have turned gray with fright. Or perhaps wrecks do as queer stunts as lightning. Friend of mine once was struck by lightning; he and the caddy had taken refuge under a tree. After the flash, when they recovered consciousness, there was my friend in the caddy's clothes, and the caddy in his. And as my friend was a large man and the caddy a very small boy—"

McKnight's story was interrupted by the indignant slam of the dining-room door. He was obliged to wait some time, and even his eternal cheerfulness was ebbing when he finally got the hospital.

"Is Doctor Van Kirk there?" he asked. "Not there? Well, can you tell me how the patient is whom Doctor Williams, from Washington, operated on last night? Well, I'm glad of that. Is she conscious? Do you happen to know her name? Yes, I'll hold the line." There was a long pause, then McKnight's voice:

"Hello—yes. Thank you very much. Good-by."

He came up-stairs, two steps at a time.

"Look here," he said, bursting into the room, "there may be something in your theory, after all. The woman's name—it may be a coincidence, but it's curious—her name is Sullivan."

"What did I tell you?" I said, sitting up suddenly in bed. "She's probably a sister of that scoundrel in lower seven, and she was afraid of what he might do."

"Well, I'll go there some day soon. She's not conscious yet. In the meantime, the only thing I can do is to keep an eye, through a detective, on the people who try to approach Bronson. We'll have the case continued, anyhow, in the hope that the stolen notes will sooner or later turn up."

"Confound this arm," I said, paying for my energy with some excruciating throbs. "There's so much to be looked after, and here I am, bandaged, splinted, and generally useless. It's a beastly shame."

"Don't forget that I am here," said McKnight pompously. "And another thing, when you feel this way just remember there are two less desirable places where you might be. One is jail, and the other is—" He strummed on an imaginary harp, with devotional eyes.

But McKnight's light-heartedness jarred on me that morning. I lay and frowned under my helplessness. When by chance I touched the little gold bag, it seemed to scorch my fingers. Richey, finding me unresponsive, left to keep his luncheon engagement with Alison West. As he clattered down the stairs, I turned my back to the morning sunshine and abandoned myself to misery. By what strain on her frayed nerves was Alison West keeping up, I wondered? Under the circumstances, would I dare to return the bag? Knowing that I had it, would she hate me for my knowledge? Or had I exaggerated the importance of the necklace, and in that case had she forgotten me already?

But McKnight had not gone, after all. I heard him coming back, his voice preceding him, and I groaned with irritation.

"Wake up!" he called. "Somebody's sent you a lot of flowers. Please hold the box, Mrs. Klopton; I'm going out to be run down by an automobile."

I roused to feeble interest. My brother's wife is punctilious about such things; all the new babies in the family have silver rattles, and all the sick people flowers.

McKnight pulled up an armful of roses, and held them out to me.

"Wonder who they're from?" he said, fumbling in the box for a card. "There's no name—yes, here's one."

He held it up and read it with exasperating slowness.

"'Best wishes for an early recovery.

A COMPANION IN MISFORTUNE.'

"Well, what do you know about that!" he exclaimed. "That's something you didn't tell me, Lollie."

"It was hardly worth mentioning," I said mendaciously, with my heart beating until I could hear it. She had not forgotten, after all.

McKnight took a bud and fastened it in his button-hole. I'm afraid I was not especially pleasant about it. They were her roses, and anyhow, they were meant for me. Richey left very soon, with an irritating final grin at the box.

"Good-by, sir woman-hater," he jeered at me from the door.

So he wore one of the roses she had sent me, to luncheon with her, and I lay back among my pillows and tried to remember that it was his game, anyhow, and that I wasn't even drawing cards. To remember that, and to forget the broken necklace under my head!

Chapter 13

FADED ROSES

I was in the house for a week. Much of that time I spent in composing and destroying letters of thanks to Miss West, and in growling at the doctor. McKnight dropped in daily, but he was less cheerful than usual. Now and then I caught him eying me as if he had something to say, but whatever it was he kept it to himself. Once during the week he went to Baltimore and saw the woman in the hospital there. From the description I had little difficulty in recognizing the young woman who had been with the murdered man in Pittsburg. But she was still unconscious. An elderly aunt had appeared, a gaunt person in black, who sat around like a buzzard on a fence, according to McKnight, and wept, in a mixed figure, into a damp handkerchief.

On the last day of my imprisonment he stopped in to thrash out a case that was coming up in court the next day, and to play a game of double solitaire with me.

"Who won the ball game?" I asked.

"We were licked. Ask me something pleasant. Oh, by the way, Bronson's out to-day."

"I'm glad I'm not on his bond," I said pessimistically. "He'll clear out."

"Not he." McKnight pounced on my ace. "He's no fool. Don't you suppose he knows you took those notes to Pittsburg? The papers were full of it. And he knows you escaped with your life and a broken arm from the wreck. What do we do next? The Commonwealth continues the case. A deaf man on a dark night would know those notes are missing."

"Don't play so fast," I remonstrated. "I have only one arm to your two. Who is trailing Bronson? Did you try to get Johnson?"

"I asked for him, but he had some work on hand."

"The murder's evidently a dead issue," I reflected. "No, I'm not joking. The wreck destroyed all the evidence. But I'm firmly convinced those notes will be offered, either to us or to Bronson very soon. Johnson's a blackguard, but he's a good detective. He could make his fortune as a game dog. What's he doing?"

McKnight put down his cards, and rising, went to the window. As he held the curtain back his customary grin looked a little forced.

"To tell you the truth, Lollie," he said, "for the last two days he has been watching a well-known Washington attorney named Lawrence Blakeley. He's across the street now."

It took a moment for me to grasp what he meant.

"Why, it's ridiculous," I asserted. "What would they trail me for? Go over and tell Johnson to get out of there, or I'll pot at him with my revolver."

"You can tell him that yourself." McKnight paused and bent forward. "Hello, here's a visitor; little man with string halt."

"I won't see him," I said firmly. "I've been bothered enough with reporters."

We listened together to Mrs. Klopton's expostulating tones in the lower hall and the creak of the boards as she came heavily up the stairs. She had a piece of paper in her hand torn from a pocket account-book, and on it was the name, "Mr. Wilson Budd Hotchkiss. Important business."

"Oh, well, show him up," I said resignedly. "You'd better put those cards away, Richey. I fancy it's the rector of the church around the corner."

But when the door opened to admit a curiously alert little man, adjusting his glasses with nervous fingers, my face must have shown my dismay.

It was the amateur detective of the Ontario!

I shook hands without enthusiasm. Here was the one survivor of the wrecked car who could do me any amount of harm. There was no hope that he had forgotten any of the incriminating details. In fact, he held in his hand the very note-book which contained them.

His manner was restrained, but it was evident he was highly excited. I introduced him to McKnight, who has the imagination I lack, and who placed him at once, mentally.

"I only learned yesterday that you had been—er—saved," he said rapidly. "Terrible accident—unspeakable. Dream about it all night and think about it all day. Broken arm?"

"No. He just wears the splint to be different from other people," McKnight drawled lazily. I glared at him: there was nothing to be gained by antagonizing the little man.

"Yes, a fractured humerus, which isn't as funny as it sounds."

"Humerus-humorous! Pretty good," he cackled. "I must say you keep up your spirits pretty well, considering everything."

"You seem to have escaped injury," I parried. He was fumbling for something in his pockets.

"Yes, I escaped," he replied abstractedly. "Remarkable thing, too. I haven't a doubt I would have broken my neck, but I landed on—you'll never guess what! I landed head first on the very pillow which was under inspection at the time of the wreck. You remember, don't you? Where did I put that package?"

He found it finally and opened it on a table, displaying with some theatricalism a rectangular piece of muslin and a similar patch of striped ticking.

"You recognize it?" he said. "The stains, you see, and the hole made by the dirk. I tried to bring away the entire pillow, but they thought I was stealing it, and made me give it up."

Richey touched the pieces gingerly. "By George," he said, "and you carry that around in your pocket! What if you should mistake it for your handkerchief?"

But Mr. Hotchkiss was not listening. He stood bent somewhat forward, leaning over the table, and fixed me with his ferret-like eyes.

"Have you see the evening papers, Mr. Blakeley?" he inquired.

I glanced to where they lay unopened, and shook my head.

"Then I have a disagreeable task," he said with evident relish. "Of course, you had considered the matter of the man Harrington's death closed, after the wreck. I did myself. As far as I was concerned, I meant to let it remain so. There were no other survivors, at least none that I knew of, and in spite of circumstances, there were a number of points in your favor."

"Thank you," I put in with a sarcasm that was lost on him.

"I verified your identity, for instance, as soon as I recovered from the shock. Also—I found on inquiring of your tailor that you invariably wore dark clothing."

McKnight came forward threateningly. "Who are you, anyhow?" he demanded. "And how is this any business of yours?" Mr. Hotchkiss was entirely unruffled.

"I have a minor position here," he said, reaching for a visiting card. "I am a very small patch on the seat of government, sir."

McKnight muttered something about certain offensive designs against the said patch and retired grumbling to the window. Our visitor was opening the paper with a tremendous expenditure of energy.

"Here it is. Listen." He read rapidly aloud:

"The Pittsburg police have sent to Baltimore two detectives who are looking up the survivors of the ill-fated Washington Flier. It has transpired that Simon Harrington, the Wood Street merchant of that city, was not killed in the wreck, but was murdered in his berth the night preceding the accident. Shortly before the collision, John Flanders, the conductor of the Flier, sent this telegram to the chief of police:

"'Body of Simon Harrington found stabbed in his berth, lower ten, Ontario, at six-thirty this morning.

JOHN FLANDERS, Conductor.'

"It is hoped that the survivors of the wrecked car Ontario will be found, to tell what they know of the discovery of the crime.

"Mr. John Gilmore, head of the steel company for which Mr. Harrington was purchasing agent, has signified his intention of sifting the matter to the bottom."

"So you see," Hotchkiss concluded, "there's trouble brewing. You and I are the only survivors of that unfortunate car."

I did not contradict him, but I knew of two others, at least: Alison West, and the woman we had left beside the road that morning, babbling incoherently, her black hair tumbling over her white face.

"Unless we can find the man who occupied lower seven," I suggested.

"I have already tried and failed. To find him would not clear you, of course, unless we could establish some connection between him and the murdered man. It is the only thing I see, however. I have learned this much," Hotchkiss concluded: "Lower seven was reserved from Cresson."

Cresson! Where Alison West and Mrs. Curtis had taken the train!

McKnight came forward and suddenly held out his hand. "Mr. Hotchkiss," he said, "I—I'm sorry if I have been offensive. I thought when you came in, that, like the Irishman and the government, you were 'forninst' us. If you will put those cheerful relics out of sight somewhere, I should be glad to have you dine with me at the Incubator." His name for his bachelor apartment. "Compared with Johnson, you are the great original protoplasm."

The strength of this was lost on Hotchkiss, but the invitation was clear. They went out together, and from my window I watched them get into McKnight's car. It was raining, and at the corner the Cannonball skidded. Across the street my detective, Johnson, looked after them with his crooked smile. As he turned up his collar he saw me, and lifted his hat.

I left the window and sat down in the growing dusk. So the occupant of lower seven had got on the car at Cresson, probably with Alison West and her companion. There was some one she cared about enough to shield. I went irritably to the door and summoned Mrs. Klopton.

"You may throw out those roses," I said without looking at her. "They are quite dead."

"They have been quite dead for three days," she retorted spitefully. "Euphemia said you threatened to dismiss her if she touched them."

Chapter 14

THE TRAP-DOOR

By Sunday evening, a week after the wreck, my inaction had goaded me to frenzy. The very sight of Johnson across the street or lurking, always within sight of the house, kept me constantly exasperated. It was on that day that things began to come to a focus, a burning-glass of events that seemed to center on me.

I dined alone that evening in no cheerful frame of mind. There had been a polo game the day before and I had lent a pony, which is always a bad thing to do. And she had wrenched her shoulder, besides helping to lose the game. There was no one in town: the temperature was ninety and climbing, and my left hand persistently cramped under its bandage.

Mrs. Klopton herself saw me served, my bread buttered and cut in tidbits, my meat ready for my fork. She hovered around me maternally, obviously trying to cheer me.

"The paper says still warmer," she ventured. "The thermometer is ninety-two now."

"And this coffee is two hundred and fifty," I said, putting down my cup. "Where is Euphemia? I haven't seen her around, or heard a dish smash all day."

"Euphemia is in bed," Mrs. Klopton said gravely. "Is your meat cut small enough, Mr. Lawrence?" Mrs. Klopton can throw more mystery into an ordinary sentence than any one I know. She can say, "Are your sheets damp, sir?" And I can tell from her tone that the house across the street has been robbed, or that my left hand neighbor has appendicitis. So now I looked up and asked the question she was waiting for.

"What's the matter with Euphemia?" I inquired idly.

"Frightened into her bed," Mrs. Klopton said in a stage whisper. "She's had three hot water bottles and she hasn't done a thing all day but moan."

"She oughtn't to take hot water bottles," I said in my severest tone. "One would make me moan. You need not wait, I'll ring if I need anything."

Mrs. Klopton sailed to the door, where she stopped and wheeled indignantly. "I only hope you won't laugh on the wrong side of your face some morning, Mr. Lawrence," she declared, with Christian fortitude. "But I warn you, I am going to have the police watch that house next door."

I was half inclined to tell her that both it and we were under police surveillance at that moment. But I like Mrs. Klopton, in spite of the fact that I make her life a torment for her, so I refrained.

"Last night, when the paper said it was going to storm, I sent Euphemia to the roof to bring the rugs in. Eliza had slipped out, although it was her evening in. Euphemia went up to the roof—it was eleven o'clock—and soon I heard her running down-stairs crying. When she got to my room she just folded up on the floor. She said there was a black figure sitting on the parapet of the house next door—the empty house—and that when she appeared it rose and waved long black arms at her and spit like a cat."

I had finished my dinner and was lighting a cigarette. "If there was any one up there, which I doubt, they probably sneezed," I suggested. "But if you feel uneasy, I'll take a look around the roof to-night before I turn in. As far as Euphemia goes, I wouldn't be uneasy about her—doesn't she always have an attack of some sort when Eliza rings in an extra evening on her?"

So I made a superficial examination of the window locks that night, visiting parts of the house that I had not seen since I bought it. Then I went to the roof. Evidently it had not been intended for any purpose save to cover the house, for unlike the houses around, there was no staircase. A ladder and a trap-door led to it, and it required some nice balancing on my part to get up with my useless arm. I made it, however, and found this unexplored part of my domain rather attractive. It was cooler than down-stairs, and I sat on the brick parapet and smoked my final cigarette. The roof of the empty house adjoined mine along the back wing, but investigation showed that the trap-door across the low dividing wall was bolted underneath.

There was nothing out of the ordinary anywhere, and so I assured Mrs. Klopton. Needless to say, I did not tell her that I had left the trap-door open, to see if it would improve the temperature of the house. I went to bed at midnight, merely because there was nothing else to do. I turned on the night lamp at the head of my bed, and picked up a volume of Shaw at random it was Arms and the Man, and I remember thinking grimly that I was a good bit of a chocolate cream soldier myself, and prepared to go to sleep. Shaw always puts me to sleep. I have no apologies to make for what occurred that night, and not even an explanation that I am sure of. I did a foolish thing under impulse, and I have not been sorry.

It was something after two when the door-bell rang. It rang quickly, twice. I got up drowsily, for the maids and Mrs. Klopton always lock themselves beyond reach of the bell at night, and put on a dressing-gown. The bell rang again on my way down-stairs. I lit the hall light and opened the door. I was wide-awake now, and I saw that it was Johnson. His bald head shone in the light—his crooked mouth was twisted in a smile.

"Good Heavens, man," I said irritably. "Don't you ever go home and go to bed?"

He closed the vestibule door behind him and cavalierly turned out the light. Our dialogue was sharp, staccato.

"Have you a key to the empty house next door?" he demanded. "Somebody's in there, and the latch is caught."

"The houses are alike. The key to this door may fit. Did you see them go in?"

"No. There's a light moving up from room to room. I saw something like it last night, and I have been watching. The patrolman reported queer doings there a week or so ago."

"A light!" I exclaimed. "Do you mean that you—"

"Very likely," he said grimly. "Have you a revolver?"

"All kinds in the gun rack," I replied, and going into the den, I came back with a Smith and Wesson. "I'm not much use," I explained, "with this arm, but I'll do what I can. There may be somebody there. The servants here have been uneasy."

Johnson planned the campaign. He suggested on account of my familiarity with the roof, that I go there and cut off escape in that direction. "I have Robison out there now—the patrolman on the beat," he said. "He'll watch below and you above, while I search the house. Be as quiet as possible."

I was rather amused. I put on some clothes and felt my way carefully up the stairs, the revolver swinging free in my pocket, my hand on the rail. At the foot of the ladder I stopped and looked up. Above me there was a gray rectangle of sky dotted with stars. It occurred to me that with my one serviceable hand holding the ladder, I was hardly in a position to defend myself, that I was about to hoist a body that I am rather careful of into a danger I couldn't see and wasn't particularly keen about anyhow. I don't mind saying that the seconds it took me to scramble up the ladder were among the most unpleasant that I recall.

I got to the top, however, without incident. I could see fairly well after the darkness of the house beneath, but there was nothing suspicious in sight. The roofs, separated by two feet of brick wall, stretched around me, unbroken save by an occasional chimney. I went very softly over to the other trap, the one belonging to the suspected house. It was closed, but I imagined I could hear Johnson's footsteps ascending heavily. Then even that was gone. A near-by clock struck three as I stood waiting. I examined my revolver then, for the first time, and found it was empty!

I had been rather skeptical until now. I had had the usual tolerant attitude of the man who is summoned from his bed to search for burglars, combined with the artificial courage of firearms. With the discovery of my empty gun, I felt like a man on the top of a volcano in lively eruption. Suddenly I found myself staring incredulously at the trap-door at my feet. I had examined it early in the evening and found it bolted. Did I imagine it, or had it raised about an inch? Wasn't it moving slowly as I looked? No, I am not a hero: I was startled almost into a panic. I had one arm, and whoever was raising that trap-door had two. My knees had a queer inclination to bend the wrong way.

Johnson's footsteps were distinct enough, but he was evidently far below. The trap, raised perhaps two inches now, remained stationary. There was no sound from beneath it: once I thought I heard two or three gasping respirations: I am not sure they were not my own. I wanted desperately to stand on one leg at a time and hold the other up out of focus of a possible revolver.

I did not see the hand appear. There was nothing there, and then it was there, clutching the frame of the trap. I did the only thing I could think of; I put my foot on it!

There was not a sound from beneath. The next moment I was kneeling and had clutched the wrist just above the hand. After a second's struggle, the arm was still. With something real to face, I was myself again.

"Don't move, or I'll stand on the trap and break your arm," I panted. What else could I threaten? I couldn't shoot, I couldn't even fight. "Johnson!" I called.

And then I realized the thing that stayed with me for a month, the thing I can not think of even now without a shudder. The hand lay ice cold, strangely quiescent. Under my fingers, an artery was beating feebly. The wrist was as slender as—I held the hand to the light. Then I let it drop.

"Good Lord," I muttered, and remained on my knees, staring at the spot where the hand had been. It was gone now: there was a faint rustle in the darkness below, and then silence.

I held up my own hand in the starlight and stared at a long scratch in the palm. "A woman!" I said to myself stupidly. "By all that's ridiculous, a woman!"

Johnson was striking matches below and swearing softly to himself. "How the devil do you get to the roof?" he called. "I think I've broken my nose."

He found the ladder after a short search and stood at the bottom, looking up at me. "Well, I suppose you haven't seen him?" he inquired. "There are enough darned cubbyholes in this house to hide a patrol wagon load of thieves." He lighted a fresh match. "Hello, here's another door!"

By the sound of his diminishing footsteps I supposed it was a rear staircase. He came up again in ten minutes or so, this time with the policeman.

"He's gone, all right," he said ruefully. "If you'd been attending to your business, Robison, you'd have watched the back door."

"I'm not twins." Robison was surly.

"Well," I broke in, as cheerfully as I could, "if you are through with this jolly little affair, and can get down my ladder without having my housekeeper ring the burglar alarm, I have some good Monongahela whisky—eh?"

They came without a second invitation across the roof, and with them safely away from the house I breathed more freely. Down in the den I fulfilled my promise, which Johnson drank to the toast, "Coming through the rye." He examined my gun rack with the eye of a connoisseur, and even when he was about to go he cast a loving eye back at the weapons.

"Ever been in the army?" he inquired.

"No," I said with a bitterness that he noticed but failed to comprehend. "I'm a chocolate cream soldier—you don't read Shaw, I suppose, Johnson?"

"Never heard of him," the detective said indifferently. "Well, good night, Mr. Blakeley. Much obliged." At the door he hesitated and coughed.

"I suppose you understand, Mr. Blakeley," he said awkwardly, "that this—er—surveillance is all in the day's work. I don't like it, but it's duty. Every man to his duty, sir."

"Sometime when you are in an open mood, Johnson," I returned, "you can explain why I am being watched at all."

Chapter 15

THE CINEMATOGRAPH

On Monday I went out for the first time. I did not go to the office. I wanted to walk. I thought fresh air and exercise would drive away the blue devils that had me by the throat. McKnight insisted on a long day in his car, but I refused.

"I don't know why not," he said sulkily. "I can't walk. I haven't walked two consecutive blocks in three years. Automobiles have made legs mere ornaments—and some not even that. We could have Johnson out there chasing us over the country at five dollars an hour!"

"He can chase us just as well at five miles an hour," I said. "But what gets me, McKnight, is why I am under surveillance at all. How do the police know I was accused of that thing?"

"The young lady who sent the flowers—she isn't likely to talk, is she?"

"No. That is, I didn't say it was a lady." I groaned as I tried to get my splinted arm into a coat. "Anyhow, she didn't tell," I finished with conviction, and McKnight laughed.

It had rained in the early morning, and Mrs. Klopton predicted more showers. In fact, so firm was her belief and so determined her eye that I took the umbrella she proffered me.

"Never mind," I said. "We can leave it next door; I have a story to tell you, Richey, and it requires proper setting."

McKnight was puzzled, but he followed me obediently round to the kitchen entrance of the empty house. It was unlocked, as I had expected. While we climbed to the upper floor I retailed the events of the previous night.

"It's the finest thing I ever heard of," McKnight said, staring up at the ladder and the trap. "What a vaudeville skit it would make! Only you ought not to have put your foot on her hand. They don't do it in the best circles."

I wheeled on him impatiently.

"You don't understand the situation at all, Richey!" I exclaimed. "What would you say if I tell you it was the hand of a lady? It was covered with rings."

"A lady!" he repeated. "Why, I'd say it was a darned compromising situation, and that the less you say of it the better. Look here, Lawrence, I think you dreamed it. You've been in the house too much. I take it all back: you do need exercise."

"She escaped through this door, I suppose," I said as patiently as I could. "Evidently down the back staircase. We might as well go down that way."

"According to the best precedents in these affairs, we should find a glove about here," he said as we started down. But he was more impressed than he cared to own. He examined the dusty steps carefully, and once, when a bit of loose plaster fell just behind him, he started like a nervous woman.

"What I don't understand is why you let her go," he said, stopping once, puzzled. "You're not usually quixotic."

"When we get out into the country, Richey," I replied gravely, "I am going to tell you another story, and if you don't tell me I'm a fool and a craven, on the strength of it, you are no friend of mine."

We stumbled through the twilight of the staircase into the blackness of the shuttered kitchen. The house had the moldy smell of closed buildings: even on that warm September morning it was damp and chilly. As we stepped into the sunshine McKnight gave a shiver.

"Now that we are out," he said, "I don't mind telling you that I have been there before. Do you remember the night you left, and, the face at the window?"

"When you speak of it—yes."

"Well, I was curious about that thing," he went on, as we started up the street, "and I went back. The street door was unlocked, and I examined every room. I was Mrs. Klopton's ghost that carried a light, and clumb."

"Did you find anything?"

"Only a clean place rubbed on the window opposite your dressing-room. Splendid view of an untidy interior. If that house is ever occupied, you'd better put stained glass in that window of yours."

As we turned the corner I glanced back. Half a block behind us Johnson was moving our way slowly. When he saw me he stopped and proceeded with great deliberation to light a cigar. By hurrying, however, he caught the car that we took, and stood unobtrusively on the rear platform. He looked fagged, and absent-mindedly paid our fares, to McKnight's delight.

"We will give him a run for his money," he declared, as the car moved countryward. "Conductor, let us off at the muddiest lane you can find."

At one o'clock, after a six-mile ramble, we entered a small country hotel. We had seen nothing of Johnson for a half hour. At that time he was a quarter of a mile behind us, and losing rapidly. Before we had finished our luncheon he staggered into the inn. One of his boots was under his arm, and his whole appearance was deplorable. He was coated with mud, streaked with perspiration, and he limped as he walked. He chose a table not far from us and ordered Scotch. Beyond touching his hat he paid no attention to us.

"I'm just getting my second wind," McKnight declared. "How do you feel, Mr. Johnson? Six or eight miles more and we'll all enjoy our dinners." Johnson put down the glass he had raised to his lips without replying.

The fact was, however, that I was like Johnson. I was soft from my week's inaction, and I was pretty well done up. McKnight, who was a well spring of vitality and high spirits, ordered a strange concoction, made of nearly everything in the bar, and sent it over to the detective, but Johnson refused it.

"I hate that kind of person," McKnight said pettishly. "Kind of a fellow that thinks you're going to poison his dog if you offer him a bone."

When we got back to the car line, with Johnson a draggled and drooping tail to the kite, I was in better spirits. I had told McKnight the story of the three hours just after the wreck; I had not named the girl, of course; she had my promise of secrecy. But I told him everything else. It was a relief to have a fresh mind on it: I had puzzled so much over the incident at the farm-house, and the necklace in the gold bag, that I had lost perspective.

He had been interested, but inclined to be amused, until I came to the broken chain. Then he had whistled softly.

"But there are tons of fine gold chains made every year," he said. "Why in the world do you think that the—er—smeary piece came from that necklace?"

I had looked around. Johnson was far behind, scraping the mud off his feet with a piece of stick.

"I have the short end of the chain in the sealskin bag," I reminded him. "When I couldn't sleep this morning I thought I would settle it, one way or the other. It was hell to go along the way I had been doing. And—there's no doubt about it, Rich. It's the same chain."

We walked along in silence until we caught the car back to town.

"Well," he said finally, "you know the girl, of course, and I don't. But if you like her—and I think myself you're rather hard hit, old man—I wouldn't give a whoop about the chain in the gold purse. It's just one of the little coincidences that hang people now and then. And as for last night—if she's the kind of a girl you say she is, and you think she had anything to do with that, you—you're addled, that's all. You can depend on it, the lady of the empty house last week is the lady of last night. And yet your train acquaintance was in Altoona at that time."

Just before we got off the car, I reverted to the subject again. It was never far back in my mind.

"About the—young lady of the train, Rich," I said, with what I suppose was elaborate carelessness, "I don't want you to get a wrong impression. I am rather unlikely to see her again, but even if I do, I—I believe she is already 'bespoke,' or next thing to it."

He made no reply, but as I opened the door with my latch-key he stood looking up at me from the pavement with his quizzical smile.

"Love is like the measles," he orated. "The older you get it, the worse the attack."

Johnson did not appear again that day. A small man in a raincoat took his place. The next morning I made my initial trip to the office, the raincoat still on hand. I had a short conference with Miller, the district attorney, at eleven. Bronson was under surveillance, he said, and any attempt to sell the notes to him would probably result in their recovery. In the meantime, as I knew, the Commonwealth had continued the case, in hope of such contingency.

At noon I left the office and took a veterinarian to see Candida, the injured pony. By one o'clock my first day's duties were performed, and a long Sahara of hot afternoon stretched ahead. McKnight, always glad to escape from the grind, suggested a vaudeville, and in sheer ennui I consented. I could neither ride, drive nor golf, and my own company bored me to distraction.

"Coolest place in town these days," he declared. "Electric fans, breezy songs, airy costumes. And there's Johnson just behind—the coldest proposition in Washington."

He gravely bought three tickets and presented the detective with one. Then we went in. Having lived a normal, busy life, the theater in the afternoon is to me about on a par with ice-cream for breakfast. Up on the stage a very stout woman in short pink skirts, with a smile that McKnight declared looked like a slash in a roll of butter, was singing nasally, with a laborious kick at the end of each verse. Johnson, two rows ahead, went to sleep. McKnight prodded me with his elbow.

"Look at the first box to the right," he said, in a stage whisper. "I want you to come over at the end of this act."

It was the first time I had seen her since I put her in the cab at Baltimore. Outwardly I presume I was calm, for no one turned to stare at me, but every atom of me cried out at the sight of her. She was leaning, bent forward, lips slightly parted, gazing raptly at the Japanese conjurer who had replaced what McKnight disrespectfully called the Columns of Hercules. Compared with the draggled lady of the farm-house, she was radiant.

For that first moment there was nothing but joy at the sight of her. McKnight's touch on my arm brought me back to reality.

"Come over and meet them," he said. "That's the cousin Miss West is visiting, Mrs. Dallas."

But I would not go. After he went I sat there alone, painfully conscious that I was being pointed out and stared at from the box. The abominable Japanese gave way to yet more atrocious performing dogs.

"How many offers of marriage will the young lady in the box have?" The dog stopped sagely at 'none,' and then pulled out a card that said eight. Wild shouts of glee by the audience. "The fools," I muttered.

After a little I glanced over. Mrs. Dallas was talking to McKnight, but She was looking straight at me. She was flushed, but more calm than I, and she did not bow. I fumbled for my hat, but the next moment I saw that they were going, and I sat still. When McKnight came back he was triumphant.

"I've made an engagement for you," he said. "Mrs. Dallas asked me to bring you to dinner to-night, and I said I knew you would fall all over yourself to go. You are requested to bring along the broken arm, and any other souvenirs of the wreck that you may possess."

"I'll do nothing of the sort," I declared, struggling against my inclination. "I can't even tie my necktie, and I have to have my food cut for me."

"Oh, that's all right," he said easily. "I'll send Stogie over to fix you up, and Mrs. Dal knows all about the arm. I told her."

Stogie is his Japanese factotum, so called because he is lean, a yellowish brown in color, and because he claims to have been shipped into this country in a box.

The Cinematograph was finishing the program. The house was dark and the music had stopped, as it does in the circus just before somebody risks his neck at so much a neck in the Dip of Death, or the hundred-foot dive. Then, with a sort of shock, I saw on the white curtain the announcement:

THE NEXT PICTURE

IS THE DOOMED WASHINGTON FLIER, TAKEN A SHORT DISTANCE FROM THE SCENE OF THE WRECK ON THE FATAL MORNING OF SEPTEMBER TENTH. TWO MILES FARTHER ON IT MET WITH ALMOST COMPLETE ANNIHILATION.

I confess to a return of some of the sickening sensations of the wreck; people around me were leaning forward with tense faces. Then the letters were gone, and I saw a long level stretch of track, even the broken stone between the ties standing out distinctly. Far off under a cloud of smoke a small object was rushing toward us and growing larger as it came.

Now it was on us, a mammoth in size, with huge drivers and a colossal tender. The engine leaped aside, as if just in time to save us from destruction, with a glimpse of a stooping fireman and a grimy engineer. The long train of sleepers followed. From a forward vestibule a porter in a white coat waved his hand. The rest of the cars seemed still wrapped in slumber. With mixed sensations I saw my own car, Ontario, fly past, and then I rose to my feet and gripped McKnight's shoulder.

On the lowest step at the last car, one foot hanging free, was a man. His black derby hat was pulled well down to keep it from blowing away, and his coat was flying open in the wind. He was swung well out from the car, his free hand gripping a small valise, every muscle tense for a jump.

"Good God, that's my man!" I said hoarsely, as the audience broke into applause. McKnight half rose: in his seat ahead Johnson stifled a yawn and turned to eye me.

I dropped into my chair limply, and tried to control my excitement. "The man on the last platform of the train," I said. "He was just about to leap; I'll swear that was my bag."

"Could you see his face?" McKnight asked in an undertone. "Would you know him again?"

"No. His hat was pulled down and his head was bent I'm going back to find out where that picture was taken. They say two miles, but it may have been forty."

The audience, busy with its wraps, had not noticed. Mrs. Dallas and Alison West had gone. In front of us Johnson had dropped his hat and was stooping for it.

"This way," I motioned to McKnight, and we wheeled into the narrow passage beside us, back of the boxes. At the end there was a door leading into the wings, and as we went boldly through I turned the key.

The final set was being struck, and no one paid any attention to us. Luckily they were similarly indifferent to a banging at the door I had locked, a banging which, I judged, signified Johnson.

"I guess we've broken up his interference," McKnight chuckled.

Stage hands were hurrying in every direction; pieces of the side wall of the last drawing-room menaced us; a switchboard behind us was singing like a tea-kettle. Everywhere we stepped we were in somebody's way. At last we were across, confronting a man in his shirt sleeves, who by dots and dashes of profanity seemed to be directing the chaos.

"Well?" he said, wheeling on us. "What can I do for you?"

"I would like to ask," I replied, "if you have any idea just where the last cinematograph picture was taken."

"Broken board—picnickers—lake?"

"No. The Washington Flier."

He glanced at my bandaged arm.

"The announcement says two miles," McKnight put in, "but we should like to know whether it is railroad miles, automobile miles, or policeman miles."

"I am sorry I can't tell you," he replied, more civilly. "We get those pictures by contract. We don't take them ourselves."

"Where are the company's offices?"

"New York." He stepped forward and grasped a super by the shoulder. "What in blazes are you doing with that gold chair in a kitchen set? Take that piece of pink plush there and throw it over a soap box, if you haven't got a kitchen chair."

I had not realized the extent of the shock, but now I dropped into a chair and wiped my forehead. The unexpected glimpse of Alison West, followed almost immediately by the revelation of the picture, had left me limp and unnerved. McKnight was looking at his watch.

"He says the moving picture people have an office down-town. We can make it if we go now."

So he called a cab, and we started at a gallop. There was no sign of the detective. "Upon my word," Richey said, "I feel lonely without him."

The people at the down-town office of the cinematograph company were very obliging. The picture had been taken, they said, at M-, just two miles beyond the scene of the wreck. It was not much, but it was something to work on. I decided not to go home, but to send McKnight's Jap for my clothes, and to dress at the Incubator. I was determined, if possible, to make my next day's investigations without Johnson. In the meantime, even if it was for the last time, I would see Her that night. I gave Stogie a note for Mrs. Klopton, and with my dinner clothes there came back the gold bag, wrapped in tissue paper.

Chapter 16

THE SHADOW OF A GIRL

Certain things about the dinner at the Dallas house will always be obscure to me. Dallas was something in the Fish Commission, and I remember his reeling off fish eggs in billions while we ate our caviar. He had some particular stunt he had been urging the government to for years—something about forbidding the establishment of mills and factories on river-banks—it seems they kill the fish, either the smoke, or the noise, or something they pour into the water.

Mrs. Dallas was there, I think. Of course, I suppose she must have been; and there was a woman in yellow: I took her in to dinner, and I remember she loosened my clams for me so I could get them. But the only real person at the table was a girl across in white, a sublimated young woman who was as brilliant as I was stupid, who never by any chance looked directly at me, and who appeared and disappeared across the candles and orchids in a sort of halo of radiance.

When the dinner had progressed from salmon to roast, and the conversation had done the same thing—from fish to scandal—the yellow gown turned to me. "We have been awfully good, haven't we, Mr. Blakeley?" she asked. "Although I am crazy to hear, I have not said 'wreck' once. I'm sure you must feel like the survivor of Waterloo, or something of the sort."

"If you want me to tell you about the wreck," I said, glancing across the table, "I'm sorry to be disappointing, but I don't remember anything."

"You are fortunate to be able to forget it." It was the first word Miss West had spoken directly to me, and it went to my head.

"There are some things I have not forgotten," I said, over the candles. "I recall coming to myself some time after, and that a girl, a beautiful girl—"

"Ah!" said the lady in yellow, leaning forward breathlessly. Miss West was staring at me coldly, but, once started, I had to stumble on.

"That a girl was trying to rouse me, and that she told me I had been on fire twice already." A shudder went around the table.

"But surely that isn't the end of the story," Mrs. Dallas put in aggrievedly. "Why, that's the most tantalizing thing I ever heard."

"I'm afraid that's all," I said. "She went her way and I went mine. If she recalls me at all, she probably thinks of me as a weak-kneed individual who faints like a woman when everything is over."

"What did I tell you?" Mrs. Dallas asserted triumphantly. "He fainted, did you hear? when everything was over! He hasn't begun to tell it."

I would have given a lot by that time if I had not mentioned the girl. But McKnight took it up there and carried it on.

"Blakeley is a regular geyser," he said. "He never spouts until he reaches the boiling point. And by that same token, although he hasn't said much about the Lady of the Wreck, I think he is crazy about her. In fact, I am sure of it. He thinks he has locked his secret in the caves of his soul, but I call you to witness that he has it nailed to his face. Look at him!"

I squirmed miserably and tried to avoid the startled eyes of the girl across the table. I wanted to choke McKnight and murder the rest of the party.

"It isn't fair," I said as coolly as I could. "I have my fingers crossed; you are five against one."

"And to think that there was a murder on that very train," broke in the lady in yellow. "It was a perfect crescendo of horrors, wasn't it? And what became of the murdered man, Mr. Blakeley?"

McKnight had the sense to jump into the conversation and save my reply.

"They say good Pittsburgers go to Atlantic City when they die," he said. "So—we are reasonably certain the gentleman did not go to the seashore."

The meal was over at last, and once in the drawing-room it was clear we hung heavy on the hostess' hands. "It is so hard to get people for bridge in September," she wailed, "there is absolutely nobody in town. Six is a dreadful number."

"It's a good poker number," her husband suggested.

The matter settled itself, however. I was hopeless, save as a dummy; Miss West said it was too hot for cards, and went out on a balcony that overlooked the Mall. With obvious relief Mrs. Dallas had the card-table brought, and I was face to face with the minute I had dreaded and hoped for for a week.

Now it had come, it was more difficult than I had anticipated. I do not know if there was a moon, but there was the urban substitute for it—the arc light. It threw the shadow of the balcony railing in long black bars against her white gown, and as it swung sometimes her face was in the light. I drew a chair close so that I could watch her.

"Do you know," I said, when she made no effort at speech, "that you are a much more formidable person to-night, in that gown, than you were the last time I saw you?"

The light swung on her face; she was smiling faintly. "The hat with the green ribbons!" she said. "I must take it back; I had almost forgotten."

"I have not forgotten—anything." I pulled myself up short. This was hardly loyalty to Richey. His voice came through the window just then, and perhaps I was wrong, but I thought she raised her head to listen.

"Look at this hand," he was saying. "Regular pianola: you could play it with your feet."

"He's a dear, isn't he?" Alison said unexpectedly. "No matter how depressed and downhearted I am, I always cheer up when I see Richey."

"He's more than that," I returned warmly. "He is the most honorable fellow I know. If he wasn't so much that way, he would have a career before him. He wanted to put on the doors of our offices, Blakeley and McKnight, P. B. H., which is Poor But Honest."

From my comparative poverty to the wealth of the girl beside me was a single mental leap. From that wealth to the grandfather who was responsible for it was another.

"I wonder if you know that I had been to Pittsburg to see your grandfather when I met you?" I said.

"You?" She was surprised.

"Yes. And you remember the alligator bag that I told you was exchanged for the one you cut off my arm?" She nodded expectantly. "Well, in that valise were the forged Andy Bronson notes, and Mr. Gilmore's deposition that they were forged."

She was on her feet in an instant. "In that bag!" she cried. "Oh, why didn't you tell me that before? Oh, it's so ridiculous, so—so hopeless. Why, I could—"

She stopped suddenly and sat down again. "I do not know that I am sorry, after all," she said after a pause. "Mr. Bronson was a friend of my father's. I—I suppose it was a bad thing for you, losing the papers?"

"Well, it was not a good thing," I conceded. "While we are on the subject of losing things, do you remember—do you know that I still have your gold purse?"

She did not reply at once. The shadow of a column was over her face, but I guessed that she was staring at me.

"You have it!" She almost whispered.

"I picked it up in the street car," I said, with a cheerfulness I did not feel. "It looks like a very opulent little purse."

Why didn't she speak about the necklace? For just a careless word to make me sane again!

"You!" she repeated, horror-stricken. And then I produced the purse and held it out on my palm. "I should have sent it to you before, I suppose, but, as you know, I have been laid up since the wreck."

We both saw McKnight at the same moment. He had pulled the curtains aside and was standing looking out at us. The tableau of give and take was unmistakable; the gold purse, her outstretched hand, my own attitude. It was over in a second; then he came out and lounged on the balcony railing.

"They're mad at me in there," he said airily, "so I came out. I suppose the reason they call it bridge is because so many people get cross over it."

The heat broke up the card group soon after, and they all came out for the night breeze. I had no more words alone with Alison.

I went back to the Incubator for the night. We said almost nothing on the way home; there was a constraint between us for the first time that I could remember. It was too early for bed, and so we smoked in the living-room and tried to talk of trivial things. After a time even those failed, and we sat silent. It was McKnight who finally broached the subject.

"And so she wasn't at Seal Harbor at all."

"No."

"Do you know where she was, Lollie?"

"Somewhere near Cresson."

"And that was the purse—her purse—with the broken necklace in it?"

"Yes, it was. You understand, don't you, Rich, that, having given her my word, I couldn't tell you?"

"I understand a lot of things," he said, without bitterness.

We sat for some time and smoked. Then Richey got up and stretched himself. "I'm off to bed, old man," he said. "Need any help with that game arm of yours?"

"No, thanks," I returned.

I heard him go into his room and lock the door. It was a bad hour for me. The first shadow between us, and the shadow of a girl at that.

Chapter 17

AT THE FARM-HOUSE AGAIN

McKnight is always a sympathizer with the early worm. It was late when he appeared. Perhaps, like myself, he had not slept well. But he was apparently cheerful enough, and he made a better breakfast than I did. It was one o'clock before we got to Baltimore. After a half hour's wait we took a local for M-, the station near which the cinematograph picture had been taken.

We passed the scene of the wreck, McKnight with curiosity, I with a sickening sense of horror. Back in the fields was the little farm-house where Alison West and I had intended getting coffee, and winding away from the track, maple trees shading it on each side, was the lane where we had stopped to rest, and where I had—it seemed presumption beyond belief now—where I had tried to comfort her by patting her hand.

We got out at M-, a small place with two or three houses and a general store. The station was a one-roomed affair, with a railed-off place at the end, where a scale, a telegraph instrument and a chair constituted the entire furnishing.

The station agent was a young man with a shrewd face. He stopped hammering a piece of wood over a hole in the floor to ask where we wanted to go.

"We're not going," said McKnight, "we're coming. Have a cigar?"

The agent took it with an inquiring glance, first at it and then at us.

"We want to ask you a few questions," began McKnight, perching himself on the railing and kicking the chair forward for me. "Or, rather, this gentleman does."

"Wait a minute," said the agent, glancing through the window. "There's a hen in that crate choking herself to death."

He was back in a minute, and took up his position near a sawdust-filled box that did duty as a cuspidor.

"Now fire away," he said.

"In the first place," I began, "do you remember the day the Washington Flier was wrecked below here?"

"Do I!" he said. "Did Jonah remember the whale?"

"Were you on the platform here when the first section passed?"

"I was."

"Do you recall seeing a man hanging to the platform of the last car?"

"There was no one hanging there when she passed here," he said with conviction. "I watched her out of sight."

"Did you see anything that morning of a man about my size, carrying a small grip, and wearing dark clothes and a derby hat?" I asked eagerly.

McKnight was trying to look unconcerned, but I was frankly anxious. It was clear that the man had jumped somewhere in the mile of track just beyond.

"Well, yes, I did." The agent cleared his throat. "When the smash came the operator at MX sent word along the wire, both ways. I got it here, and I was pretty near crazy, though I knew it wasn't any fault of mine.

"I was standing on the track looking down, for I couldn't leave the office, when a young fellow with light hair limped up to me and asked me what that smoke was over there.

"'That's what's left of the Washington Flier,' I said, 'and I guess there's souls going up in that smoke.'

"'Do you mean the first section?' he said, getting kind of greenish-yellow.

"'That's what I mean,' I said; 'split to kindling wood because Rafferty, on the second section, didn't want to be late.'

"He put his hand out in front of him, and the satchel fell with a bang.

"'My God!' he said, and dropped right on the track in a heap.

"I got him into the station and he came around, but he kept on groaning something awful. He'd sprained his ankle, and when he got a little better I drove him over in Carter's milk wagon to the Carter place, and I reckon he stayed there a spell."

"That's all, is it?" I asked.

"That's all—or, no, there's something else. About noon that day one of the Carter twins came down with a note from him asking me to send a long-distance message to some one in Washington."

"To whom?" I asked eagerly.

"I reckon I've forgot the name, but the message was that this fellow—Sullivan was his name—was at M-, and if the man had escaped from the wreck would he come to see him."

"He wouldn't have sent that message to me," I said to McKnight, rather crestfallen. "He'd have every object in keeping out of my way."

"There might be reasons," McKnight observed judicially. "He might not have found the papers then."

"Was the name Blakeley?" I asked.

"It might have been—I can't say. But the man wasn't there, and there was a lot of noise. I couldn't hear well. Then in half an hour down came the other twin to say the gentleman was taking on awful and didn't want the message sent."

"He's gone, of course?"

"Yes. Limped down here in about three days and took the noon train for the city."

It seemed a certainty now that our man, having hurt himself somewhat in his jump, had stayed quietly in the farm-house until he was able to travel. But, to be positive, we decided to visit the Carter place.

I gave the station agent a five-dollar bill, which he rolled up with a couple of others and stuck in his pocket. I turned as we got to a bend in the road, and he was looking curiously after us.

It was not until we had climbed the hill and turned onto the road to the Carter place that I realized where we were going. Although we approached it from another direction, I knew the farm-house at once. It was the one where Alison West and I had breakfasted nine days before. With the new restraint between us, I did not tell McKnight. I wondered afterward if he had suspected it. I saw him looking hard at the gate-post which had figured in one of our mysteries, but he asked no questions. Afterward he grew almost taciturn, for him, and let me do most of the talking.

We opened the front gate of the Carter place and went slowly up the walk. Two ragged youngsters, alike even to freckles and squints, were playing in the yard.

"Is your mother around?" I asked.

"In the front room. Walk in," they answered in identical tones.

As we got to the porch we heard voices, and stopped. I knocked, but the people within, engaged in animated, rather one-sided conversation, did not answer.

"'In the front room. Walk in,'" quoted McKnight, and did so.

In the stuffy farm parlor two people were sitting. One, a pleasant-faced woman with a checked apron, rose, somewhat embarrassed, to meet us. She did not know me, and I was thankful. But our attention was riveted on a little man who was sitting before a table, writing busily. It was Hotchkiss!

He got up when he saw us, and had the grace to look uncomfortable.

"Such an interesting case," he said nervously, "I took the liberty—"

"Look here," said McKnight suddenly, "did you make any inquiries at the station?"

"A few," he confessed. "I went to the theater last night—I felt the need of a little relaxation—and the sight of a picture there, a cinematograph affair, started a new line of thought. Probably the same clue brought you gentlemen. I learned a good bit from the station agent."

"The son-of-a-gun," said McKnight. "And you paid him, I suppose?"

"I gave him five dollars," was the apologetic answer. Mrs. Carter, hearing sounds of strife in the yard, went out, and Hotchkiss folded up his papers.

"I think the identity of the man is established," he said. "What number of hat do you wear, Mr. Blakeley?"

"Seven and a quarter," I replied.

"Well, it's only piling up evidence," he said cheerfully. "On the night of the murder you wore light gray silk underclothing, with the second button of the shirt missing. Your hat had 'L. B.' in gilt letters inside, and there was a very minute hole in the toe of one black sock."

"Hush," McKnight protested. "If word gets to Mrs. Klopton that Mr. Blakeley was wrecked, or robbed, or whatever it was, with a button missing and a hole in one sock, she'll retire to the Old Ladies' Home. I've heard her threaten it."

Mr. Hotchkiss was without a sense of humor. He regarded McKnight gravely and went on:

"I've been up in the room where the man lay while he was unable to get away, and there is nothing there. But I found what may be a possible clue in the dust heap.

"Mrs. Carter tells me that in unpacking his grip the other day she took out of the coat of the pajamas some pieces of a telegram. As I figure it, the pajamas were his own. He probably had them on when he effected the exchange."

I nodded assent. All I had retained of my own clothing was the suit of pajamas I was wearing and my bath-robe.

"Therefore the telegram was his, not yours. I have pieces here, but some are missing. I am not discouraged, however."

He spread out some bits of yellow paper, and we bent over them curiously. It was something like this:

Man with p- Get-

Br-

We spelled it out slowly.

"Now," Hotchkiss announced, "I make it something like this: The 'p.-' is one of two things, pistol—you remember the little pearl-handled affair belonging to the murdered man—or it is pocket-book. I am inclined to the latter view, as the pocket-book had been disturbed and the pistol had not."

I took the piece of paper from the table and scrawled four words on it.

"Now," I said, rearranging them, "it happens, Mr. Hotchkiss, that I found one of these pieces of the telegram on the train. I thought it had been dropped by some one else, you see, but that's immaterial. Arranged this way it almost makes sense. Fill out that 'p.-' with the rest of the word, as I imagine it, and it makes 'papers,' and add this scrap and you have:

"'Man with papers in lower ten, car seven. Get them.'

McKnight slapped Hotchkiss on the back. "You're a trump," he said. "Br- is Bronson, of course. It's almost too easy. You see, Mr. Blakeley here engaged lower ten, but found it occupied by the man who was later murdered there. The man who did the thing was a friend of Bronson's, evidently, and in trying to get the papers we have the motive for the crime."

"There are still some things to be explained." Mr. Hotchkiss wiped his glasses and put them on. "For one thing, Mr. Blakeley, I am puzzled by that bit of chain."

I did not glance at McKnight. I felt that the hand, with which I was gathering up the bits of torn paper were shaking. It seemed to me that this astute little man was going to drag in the girl in spite of me.

Chapter 18

A NEW WORLD

Hotchkiss jotted down the bits of telegram and rose.

"Well," he said, "we've done something. We've found where the murderer left the train, we know what day he went to Baltimore, and, most important of all, we have a motive for the crime."

"It seems the irony of fate," said McKnight, getting up, "that a man should kill another man for certain papers he is supposed to be carrying, find he hasn't got them after all, decide to throw suspicion on another man by changing berths and getting out, bag and baggage, and then, by the merest fluke of chance, take with him, in the valise he changed for his own, the very notes he was after. It was a bit of luck for him."

"Then why," put in Hotchkiss doubtfully, "why did he collapse when he heard of the wreck? And what about the telephone message the station agent sent? You remember they tried to countermand it, and with some excitement."

"We will ask him those questions when we get him," McKnight said. We were on the unrailed front porch by that time, and Hotchkiss had put away his notebook. The mother of the twins followed us to the steps.

"Dear me," she exclaimed volubly, "and to think I was forgetting to tell you! I put the young man to bed with a spice poultice on his ankle: my mother always was a firm believer in spice poultices. It's wonderful what they will do in croup! And then I took the children and went down to see the wreck. It was Sunday, and the mister had gone to church; hasn't missed a day since he took the pledge nine years ago. And on the way I met two people, a man and a woman. They looked half dead, so I sent them right here for breakfast and some soap and water. I always say soap is better than liquor after a shock."

Hotchkiss was listening absently: McKnight was whistling under his breath, staring down across the field to where a break in the woods showed a half dozen telegraph poles, the line of the railroad.

"It must have been twelve o'clock when we got back; I wanted the children to see everything, because it isn't likely they'll ever see another wreck like that. Rows of—"

"About twelve o'clock," I broke in, "and what then?"

"The young man up-stairs was awake," she went on, "and hammering at his door like all possessed. And it was locked on the outside!" She paused to enjoy her sensation.

"I would like to see that lock," Hotchkiss said promptly, but for some reason the woman demurred.

"I will bring the key down," she said and disappeared. When she returned she held out an ordinary door key of the cheapest variety.

"We had to break the lock," she volunteered, "and the key didn't turn up for two days. Then one of the twins found the turkey gobbler trying to swallow it. It has been washed since," she hastened to assure Hotchkiss, who showed an inclination to drop it.

"You don't think he locked the door himself and threw the key out of the window?" the little man asked.

"The windows are covered with mosquito netting, nailed on. The mister blamed it on the children, and it might have been Obadiah. He's the quiet kind, and you never know what he's about."

"He's about to strangle, isn't he," McKnight remarked lazily, "or is that Obadiah?"

Mrs. Carter picked the boy up and inverted him, talking amiably all the time. "He's always doing it," she said, giving him a shake. "Whenever we miss anything we look to see if Obadiah's black in the face." She gave him another shake, and the quarter I had given him shot out as if blown from a gun. Then we prepared to go back to the station.

From where I stood I could look into the cheery farm kitchen, where Alison West and I had eaten our al fresco breakfast. I looked at the table with mixed emotions, and then, gradually, the meaning of something on it penetrated my mind. Still in its papers, evidently just opened, was a hat box, and protruding over the edge of the box was a streamer of vivid green ribbon.

On the plea that I wished to ask Mrs. Carter a few more questions, I let the others go on. I watched them down the flagstone walk; saw McKnight stop and examine the gate-posts and saw, too, the quick glance he threw back at the house. Then I turned to Mrs. Carter.

"I would like to speak to the young lady up-stairs," I said.

She threw up her hands with a quick gesture of surrender. "I've done all I could," she exclaimed. "She won't like it very well, but—she's in the room over the parlor."

I went eagerly up the ladder-like stairs, to the rag-carpeted hall. Two doors were open, showing interiors of four poster beds and high bureaus. The door of the room over the parlor was almost closed. I hesitated in the hallway: after all, what right had I to intrude on her? But she settled my difficulty by throwing open the door and facing me.

"I—I beg your pardon, Miss West," I stammered. "It has just occurred to me that I am unpardonably rude. I saw the hat down-stairs and I—I guessed—"

"The hat!" she said. "I might have known. Does Richey know I am here?"

"I don't think so." I turned to go down the stairs again. Then I halted. "The fact is," I said, in an attempt at justification, "I'm in rather a mess these days, and I'm apt to do irresponsible things. It is not impossible that I shall be arrested, in a day or so, for the murder of Simon Harrington."

She drew her breath in sharply. "Murder!" she echoed. "Then they have found you after all!"

"I don't regard it as anything more than—er—inconvenient," I lied. "They can't convict me, you know. Almost all the witnesses are dead."

She was not deceived for a moment. She came over to me and stood, both hands on the rail of the stair. "I know just how grave it is," she said quietly. "My grandfather will not leave one stone unturned, and he can be terrible—terrible. But"—she looked directly into my eyes as I stood below her on the stairs—"the time may come—soon—when I can help you. I'm afraid I shall not want to; I'm a dreadful coward, Mr. Blakeley. But—I will." She tried to smile.

"I wish you would let me help you," I said unsteadily. "Let us make it a bargain: each help the other!"

The girl shook her head with a sad little smile. "I am only as unhappy as I deserve to be," she said. And when I protested and took a step toward her she retreated, with her hands out before her.

"Why don't you ask me all the questions you are thinking?" she demanded, with a catch in her voice. "Oh, I know them. Or are you afraid to ask?"

I looked at her, at the lines around her eyes, at the drawn look about her mouth. Then I held out my hand. "Afraid!" I said, as she gave me hers. "There is nothing in God's green earth I am afraid of, save of trouble for you. To ask questions would be to imply a lack of faith. I ask you nothing. Some day, perhaps, you will come to me yourself and let me help you."

The next moment I was out in the golden sunshine: the birds were singing carols of joy: I walked dizzily through rainbow-colored clouds, past the twins, cherubs now, swinging on the gate. It was a new world into which I stepped from the Carter farm-house that morning, for—I had kissed her!

Chapter 19

AT THE TABLE NEXT

McKnight and Hotchkiss were sauntering slowly down the road as I caught up with them. As usual, the little man was busy with some abstruse mental problem.

"The idea is this," he was saying, his brows knitted in thought, "if a left-handed man, standing in the position of the man in the picture, should jump from a car, would he be likely to sprain his right ankle? When a right-handed man prepares for a leap of that kind, my theory is that he would hold on with his right hand, and alight at the proper time, on his right foot. Of course—"

"I imagine, although I don't know," interrupted McKnight, "that a man either ambidextrous or one-armed, jumping from the Washington Flier, would be more likely to land on his head."

"Anyhow," I interposed, "what difference does it make whether Sullivan used one hand or the other? One pair of handcuffs will put both hands out of commission."

As usual when one of his pet theories was attacked, Hotchkiss looked aggrieved.

"My dear sir," he expostulated, "don't you understand what bearing this has on the case? How was the murdered man lying when he was found?"

"On his back," I said promptly, "head toward the engine."

"Very well," he retorted, "and what then? Your heart lies under your fifth intercostal space, and to reach it a right-handed blow would have struck either down or directly in.

"But, gentleman, the point of entrance for the stiletto was below the heart, striking up! As Harrington lay with his head toward the engine, a person in the aisle must have used the left hand."

McKnight's eyes sought mine and he winked at me solemnly as I unostentatiously transferred the hat I was carrying to my right hand. Long training has largely counterbalanced heredity in my case, but I still pitch ball, play tennis and carve with my left hand. But Hotchkiss was too busy with his theories to notice me.

We were only just in time for our train back to Baltimore, but McKnight took advantage of a second's delay to shake the station agent warmly by the hand.

"I want to express my admiration for you," he said beamingly. "Ability of your order is thrown away here. You should have been a city policeman, my friend."

The agent looked a trifle uncertain.

"The young lady was the one who told me to keep still," he said.

McKnight glanced at me, gave the agent's hand a final shake, and climbed on board. But I knew perfectly that he had guessed the reason for my delay.

He was very silent on the way home. Hotchkiss, too, had little to say. He was reading over his notes intently, stopping now and then to make a penciled addition. Just before we left the train Richey turned to me. "I suppose it was the key to the door that she tied to the gate?"

"Probably. I did not ask her."

"Curious, her locking that fellow in," he reflected. "You may depend on it, there was a good reason for it all. And I wish you wouldn't be so suspicious of motives, Rich," I said warmly.

"Only yesterday you were the suspicious one," he retorted, and we lapsed into strained silence.

It was late when we got to Washington. One of Mrs. Klopton's small tyrannies was exacting punctuality at meals, and, like several other things, I respected it. There are always some concessions that should be made in return for faithful service.

So, as my dinner hour of seven was long past, McKnight and I went to a little restaurant down town where they have a very decent way of fixing chicken a la King. Hotchkiss had departed, economically bent, for a small hotel where he lived on the American plan.

"I want to think some things over," he said in response to my invitation to dinner, "and, anyhow, there's no use dining out when I pay the same, dinner or no dinner, where I am stopping."

The day had been hot, and the first floor dining-room was sultry in spite of the palms and fans which attempted to simulate the verdure and breezes of the country.

It was crowded, too, with a typical summer night crowd, and, after sitting for a few minutes in a sweltering corner, we got up and went to the smaller dining-room up-stairs. Here it was not so warm, and we settled ourselves comfortably by a window.

Over in a corner half a dozen boys on their way back to school were ragging a perspiring waiter, a proceeding so exactly to McKnight's taste that he insisted on going over to join them. But their table was full, and somehow that kind of fun had lost its point for me.

Not far from us a very stout, middle-aged man, apoplectic with the heat, was elephantinely jolly for the benefit of a bored-looking girl across the table from him, and at the next table a newspaper woman ate alone, the last edition propped against the water-bottle before her, her hat, for coolness, on the corner of the table. It was a motley Bohemian crowd.

I looked over the room casually, while McKnight ordered the meal. Then my attention was attracted to the table next to ours. Two people were sitting there, so deep in conversation that they did not notice us. The woman's face was hidden under her hat, as she traced the pattern of the cloth mechanically with her fork. But the man's features stood out clear in the light of the candles on the table. It was Bronson!

"He shows the strain, doesn't he?" McKnight said, holding up the wine list as if he read from it. "Who's the woman?"

"Search me," I replied, in the same way.

When the chicken came, I still found myself gazing now and then at the abstracted couple near me. Evidently the subject of conversation was unpleasant. Bronson was eating little, the woman not at all. Finally he got up, pushed his chair back noisily, thrust a bill at the waiter and stalked out.

The woman sat still for a moment; then, with an apparent resolution to make the best of it, she began slowly to eat the meal before her.

But the quarrel had taken away her appetite, for the mixture in our chafing-dish was hardly ready to serve before she pushed her chair back a little and looked around the room.

I caught my first glimpse of her face then, and I confess it startled me. It was the tall, stately woman of the Ontario, the woman I had last seen cowering beside the road, rolling pebbles in her hand, blood streaming from a cut over her eye. I could see the scar now, a little affair, about an inch long, gleaming red through its layers of powder.

And then, quite unexpectedly, she turned and looked directly at me. After a minute's uncertainty, she bowed, letting her eyes rest on mine with a calmly insolent stare. She glanced at McKnight for a moment, then back to me. When she looked away again I breathed easier.

"Who is it?" asked McKnight under his breath.

"Ontario." I formed it with my lips rather than said it. McKnight's eyebrows went up and he looked with increased interest at the black-gowned figure.

I ate little after that. The situation was rather bad for me, I began to see. Here was a woman who could, if she wished, and had any motive for so doing, put me in jail under a capital charge. A word from her to the police, and polite surveillance would become active interference.

Then, too, she could say that she had seen me, just after the wreck, with a young woman from the murdered man's car, and thus probably bring Alison West into the case.

It is not surprising, then, that I ate little. The woman across seemed in no hurry to go. She loitered over a demi-tasse, and that finished, sat with her elbow on the table, her chin in her hand, looking darkly at the changing groups in the room.

The fun at the table where the college boys sat began to grow a little noisy; the fat man, now a purplish shade, ambled away behind his slim companion; the newspaper woman pinned on her business-like hat and stalked out. Still the woman at the next table waited.

It was a relief when the meal was over. We got our hats and were about to leave the room, when a waiter touched me on the arm.

"I beg your pardon, sir," he said, "but the lady at the table near the window, the lady in black, sir, would like to speak to you."

I looked down between the rows of tables to where the woman sat alone, her chin still resting on her hand, her black eyes still insolently staring, this time at me.

"I'll have to go," I said to McKnight hurriedly. "She knows all about that affair and she'd be a bad enemy."

"I don't like her lamps," McKnight observed, after a glance at her. "Better jolly her a little. Good-by."

Chapter 20

THE NOTES AND A BARGAIN

I went back slowly to where the woman sat alone.

She smiled rather oddly as I drew near, and pointed to the chair Bronson had vacated.

"Sit down, Mr. Blakeley," she said, "I am going to take a few minutes of your valuable time."

"Certainly." I sat down opposite her and glanced at a cuckoo clock on the wall. "I am sorry, but I have only a few minutes. If you—" She laughed a little, not very pleasantly, and opening a small black fan covered with spangles, waved it slowly.

"The fact is," she said, "I think we are about to make a bargain."

"A bargain?" I asked incredulously. "You have a second advantage of me. You know my name"—I paused suggestively and she took the cue.

"I am Mrs. Conway," she said, and flicked a crumb off the table with an over-manicured finger.

The name was scarcely a surprise. I had already surmised that this might be the woman whom rumor credited as being Bronson's common-law wife. Rumor, I remembered, had said other things even less pleasant, things which had been brought out at Bronson's arrest for forgery.

"We met last under less fortunate circumstances," she was saying. "I have been fit for nothing since that terrible day. And you—you had a broken arm, I think."

"I still have it," I said, with a lame attempt at jocularity; "but to have escaped at all was a miracle. We have much, indeed, to be thankful for."

"I suppose we have," she said carelessly, "although sometimes I doubt it." She was looking somberly toward the door through which her late companion had made his exit.

"You sent for me—" I said.

"Yes, I sent for you." She roused herself and sat erect. "Now, Mr. Blakeley, have you found those papers?"

"The papers? What papers?" I parried. I needed time to think.

"Mr. Blakeley," she said quietly, "I think we can lay aside all subterfuge. In the first place let me refresh your mind about a few things. The Pittsburg police are looking for the survivors of the car Ontario; there are three that I know of—yourself, the young woman with whom you left the scene of the wreck, and myself. The wreck, you will admit, was a fortunate one for you."

I nodded without speaking.

"At the time of the collision you were in rather a hole," she went on, looking at me with a disagreeable smile. "You were, if I remember, accused of a rather atrocious crime. There was a lot of corroborative evidence, was there not? I seem to remember a dirk and the murdered man's pocket-book in your possession, and a few other things that were—well, rather unpleasant."

I was thrown a bit off my guard.

"You remember also," I said quickly, "that a man disappeared from the car, taking my clothes, papers and everything."

"I remember that you said so." Her tone was quietly insulting, and I bit my lip at having been caught. It was no time to make a defense.

"You have missed one calculation," I said coldly, "and that is, the discovery of the man who left the train."

"You have found him?" She bent forward, and again I regretted my hasty speech. "I knew it; I said so."

"We are going to find him," I asserted, with a confidence I did not feel. "We can produce at any time proof that a man left the Flier a few miles beyond the wreck. And we can find him, I am positive."

"But you have not found him yet?" She was clearly disappointed. "Well, so be it. Now for our bargain. You will admit that I am no fool."

I made no such admission, and she smiled mockingly.

"How flattering you are!" she said. "Very well. Now for the premises. You take to Pittsburg four notes held by the Mechanics' National Bank, to have Mr. Gilmore, who is ill, declare his indorsement of them forged.

"On the journey back to Pittsburg two things happen to you: you lose your clothing, your valise and your papers, including the notes, and you are accused of murder. In fact, Mr. Blakeley, the circumstances were most singular, and the evidence—well, almost conclusive."

I was completely at her mercy, but I gnawed my lip with irritation.

"Now for the bargain." She leaned over and lowered her voice. "A fair exchange, you know. The minute you put those four notes in my hand—that minute the blow to my head has caused complete forgetfulness as to the events of that awful morning. I am the only witness, and I will be silent. Do you understand? They will call off their dogs."

My head was buzzing with the strangeness of the idea.

"But," I said, striving to gain time, "I haven't the notes. I can't give you what I haven't got."

"You have had the case continued," she said sharply. "You expect to find them. Another thing," she added slowly, watching my face, "if you don't get them soon, Bronson will have them. They have been offered to him already, but at a prohibitive price."

"But," I said, bewildered, "what is your object in coming to me? If Bronson will get them anyhow—"

She shut her fan with a click and her face was not particularly pleasant to look at.

"You are dense," she said insolently. "I want those papers—for myself, not for Andy Bronson."

"Then the idea is," I said, ignoring her tone, "that you think you have me in a hole, and that if I find those papers and give them to you you will let me out. As I understand it, our friend Bronson, under those circumstances, will also be in a hole."

She nodded.

"The notes would be of no use to you for a limited length of time," I went on, watching her narrowly. "If they are not turned over to the state's attorney within a reasonable time there will have to be a nolle pros—that is, the case will simply be dropped for lack of evidence."

"A week would answer, I think," she said slowly. "You will do it, then?"

I laughed, although I was not especially cheerful.

"No, I'll not do it. I expect to come across the notes any time now, and I expect just as certainly to turn them over to the state's attorney when I get them."

She got up suddenly, pushing her chair back with a noisy grating sound that turned many eyes toward us.

"You're more of a fool than I thought you," she sneered, and left me at the table.

Chapter 21

Mc KNIGHT'S THEORY

I confess I was staggered. The people at the surrounding tables, after glancing curiously in my direction, looked away again.

I got my hat and went out in a very uncomfortable frame of mind. That she would inform the police at once of what she knew I never doubted, unless possibly she would give a day or two's grace in the hope that I would change my mind.

I reviewed the situation as I waited for a car. Two passed me going in the opposite direction, and on the first one I saw Bronson, his hat over his eyes, his arms folded, looking moodily ahead. Was it imagination? or was the small man huddled in the corner of the rear seat Hotchkiss?

As the car rolled on I found myself smiling. The alert little man was for all the world like a terrier, ever on the scent, and scouring about in every direction.

I found McKnight at the Incubator, with his coat off, working with enthusiasm and a manicure file over the horn of his auto.

"It's the worst horn I ever ran across," he groaned, without looking up, as I came in. "The blankety-blank thing won't blow."

He punched it savagely, finally eliciting a faint throaty croak.

"Sounds like croup," I suggested. "My sister-in-law uses camphor and goose greese for it; or how about a spice poultice?"

But McKnight never sees any jokes but his own. He flung the horn clattering into a corner, and collapsed sulkily into a chair.

"Now," I said, "if you're through manicuring that horn, I'll tell you about my talk with the lady in black."

"What's wrong?" asked McKnight languidly. "Police watching her, too?"

"Not exactly. The fact is, Rich, there's the mischief to pay."

Stogie came in, bringing a few additions to our comfort. When he went out I told my story.

"You must remember," I said, "that I had seen this woman before the morning of the wreck. She was buying her Pullman ticket when I did. Then the next morning, when the murder was discovered, she grew hysterical, and I gave her some whisky. The third and last time I saw her, until to-night, was when she crouched beside the road, after the wreck."

McKnight slid down in his chair until his weight rested on the small of his back, and put his feet on the big reading table.

"It is rather a facer," he said. "It's really too good a situation for a commonplace lawyer. It ought to be dramatized. You can't agree, of course; and by refusing you run the chance of jail, at least, and of having Alison brought into publicity, which is out of the question. You say she was at the Pullman window when you were?"

"Yes; I bought her ticket for her. Gave her lower eleven."

"And you took ten?"

"Lower ten."

McKnight straightened up and looked at me.

"Then she thought you were in lower ten."

"I suppose she did, if she thought at all."

"But listen, man." McKnight was growing excited. "What do you figure out of this? The Conway woman knows you have taken the notes to Pittsburg. The probabilities are that she follows you there, on the chance of an opportunity to get them, either for Bronson or herself.

"Nothing doing during the trip over or during the day in Pittsburg; but she learns the number of your berth as you buy it at the Pullman ticket office in Pittsburg, and she thinks she sees her chance. No one could have foreseen that that drunken fellow would have crawled into your berth.

"Now, I figure it out this way: She wanted those notes desperately—does still—not for Bronson, but to hold over his head for some purpose. In the night, when everything is quiet, she slips behind the curtains of lower ten, where the man's breathing shows he is asleep. Didn't you say he snored?"

"He did!" I affirmed. "But I tell you—"

"Now keep still and listen. She gropes cautiously around in the darkness, finally discovering the wallet under the pillow. Can't you see it yourself?"

He was leaning forward, excitedly, and I could almost see the gruesome tragedy he was depicting.

"She draws out the wallet. Then, perhaps she remembers the alligator bag, and on the possibility that the notes are there, instead of in the pocket-book, she gropes around for it. Suddenly, the man awakes and clutches at the nearest object, perhaps her neck chain, which breaks. She drops the pocket-book and tries to escape, but he has caught her right hand.

"It is all in silence; the man is still stupidly drunk. But he holds her in a tight grip. Then the tragedy. She must get away; in a minute the car will be aroused. Such a woman, on such an errand, does not go without some sort of a weapon, in this case a dagger, which, unlike a revolver, is noiseless.

"With a quick thrust—she's a big woman and a bold one—she strikes. Possibly Hotchkiss is right about the left-hand blow. Harrington may have held her right hand, or perhaps she held the dirk in her left hand as she groped with her right. Then, as the man falls back, and his grasp relaxes, she straightens and attempts to get away. The swaying of the car throws her almost into your berth, and, trembling with terror, she crouches behind the curtains of lower ten until everything is still. Then she goes noiselessly back to her berth."

I nodded.

"It seems to fit partly, at least," I said. "In the morning when she found that the crime had been not only fruitless, but that she had searched the wrong berth and killed the wrong man; when she saw me emerge, unhurt, just as she was bracing herself for the discovery of my dead body, then she went into hysterics. You remember, I gave her some whisky.

"It really seems a tenable theory. But, like the Sullivan theory, there are one or two things that don't agree with the rest. For one thing, how did the remainder of that chain get into Alison West's possession?"

"She may have picked it up on the floor."

"We'll admit that," I said; "and I'm sure I hope so. Then how did the murdered man's pocket-book get into the sealskin bag? And the dirk, how account for that, and the blood-stains?"

"Now what's the use," asked McKnight aggrievedly, "of my building up beautiful theories for you to pull down? We'll take it to Hotchkiss. Maybe he can tell from the blood-stains if the murderer's finger nails were square or pointed."

"Hotchkiss is no fool," I said warmly. "Under all his theories there's a good hard layer of common sense. And we must remember, Rich, that neither of our theories includes the woman at Doctor Van Kirk's hospital, that the charming picture you have just drawn does not account for Alison West's connection with the case, or for the bits of telegram in the Sullivan fellow's pajamas pocket. You are like the man who put the clock together; you've got half of the works left over."

"Oh, go home," said McKnight disgustedly. "I'm no Edgar Allan Poe. What's the use of coming here and asking me things if you're so particular?"

With one of his quick changes of mood, he picked up his guitar.

"Listen to this," he said. "It is a Hawaiian song about a fat lady, oh, ignorant one! and how she fell off her mule."

But for all the lightness of the words, the voice that followed me down the stairs was anything but cheery.

"There was a Kanaka in Balu did dwell,

Who had for his daughter a monstrous fat girl—

he sang in his clear tenor. I paused on the lower floor and listened. He had stopped singing as abruptly as he had begun.

Chapter 22

AT THE BOARDING-HOUSE

I had not been home for thirty-six hours, since the morning of the preceding day. Johnson was not in sight, and I let myself in quietly with my latchkey. It was almost midnight, and I had hardly settled myself in the library when the bell rang and I was surprised to find Hotchkiss, much out of breath, in the vestibule.

"Why, come in, Mr. Hotchkiss," I said. "I thought you were going home to go to bed."

"So I was, so I was." He dropped into a chair beside my reading lamp and mopped his face. "And here it is almost midnight, and I'm wider awake than ever. I've seen Sullivan, Mr. Blakeley."

"You have!"

"I have," he said impressively.

"You were following Bronson at eight o'clock. Was that when it happened?"

"Something of the sort. When I left you at the door of the restaurant, I turned and almost ran into a plain clothes man from the central office. I know him pretty well; once or twice he has taken me with him on interesting bits of work. He knows my hobby."

"You know him, too, probably. It was the man Arnold, the detective whom the state's attorney has had watching Bronson."

Johnson being otherwise occupied, I had asked for Arnold myself.

I nodded.

"Well, he stopped me at once; said he'd been on the fellow's tracks since early morning and had had no time for luncheon. Bronson, it seems, isn't eating much these days. I at once jotted down the fact, because it argued that he was being bothered by the man with the notes."

"It might point to other things," I suggested. "Indigestion, you know."

Hotchkiss ignored me. "Well, Arnold had some reason for thinking that Bronson would try to give him the slip that night, so he asked me to stay around the private entrance there while he ran across the Street and got something to eat. It seemed a fair presumption that, as he had gone there with a lady, they would dine leisurely, and Arnold would have plenty of time to get back."

"What about your own dinner?" I asked curiously.

"Sir," he said pompously, "I have given you a wrong estimate of Wilson Budd Hotchkiss if you think that a question of dinner would even obtrude itself on his mind at such a time as this."

He was a frail little man, and to-night he looked pale with heat and over-exertion.

"Did you have any luncheon?" I asked.

He was somewhat embarrassed at that.

"I—really, Mr. Blakeley, the events of the day were so engrossing—"

"Well," I said, "I'm not going to see you drop on the floor from exhaustion. Just wait a minute."

I went back to the pantry, only to be confronted with rows of locked doors and empty dishes. Downstairs, in the basement kitchen, however, I found two unattractive looking cold chops, some dry bread and a piece of cake, wrapped in a napkin, and from its surreptitious and generally hang-dog appearance, destined for the coachman in the stable at the rear. Trays there were none—everything but the chairs and tables seemed under lock and key, and there was neither napkin, knife nor fork to be found.

The luncheon was not attractive in appearance, but Hotchkiss ate his cold chops and gnawed at the crusts as though he had been famished, while he told his story.

"I had been there only a few minutes," he said, with a chop in one hand and the cake in the other, "when Bronson rushed out and cut across the street. He's a tall man, Mr. Blakeley, and I had had work keeping close. It was a relief when he jumped on a passing car, although being well behind, it was a hard run for me to catch him. He had left the lady.

"Once on the car, we simply rode from one end of the line to the other and back again. I suppose he was passing the time, for he looked at his watch now and then, and when I did once get a look at us face it made me—er—uncomfortable. He could have crushed me like a fly, sir."

I had brought Mr. Hotchkiss a glass of wine, and he was looking better. He stopped to finish it, declining with a wave of his hand to have it refilled, and continued:

"About nine o'clock or a little later he got off somewhere near Washington Circle. He went along one of the residence streets there, turned to his left a square or two, and rang a bell. He had been admitted when I got there, but I guessed from the appearance of the place that it was a boarding-house.

"I waited a few minutes and rang the bell. When a maid answered it, I asked for Mr. Sullivan. Of course there was no Mr. Sullivan there.

"I said I was sorry; that the man I was looking for was a new boarder. She was sure there was no such boarder in the house; the only new arrival was a man on the third floor—she thought his name was Stuart.

"'My friend has a cousin by that name,' I said. 'I'll just go up and see.'

"She wanted to show me up, but I said it was unnecessary. So after telling me it was the bedroom and sitting-room on the third floor front, I went up.

"I met a couple of men on the stairs, but neither of them paid any attention to me. A boarding-house is the easiest place in the world to enter."

"They're not always so easy to leave," I put in, to his evident irritation.

"When I got to the third story, I took out a bunch of keys and posted myself by a door near the ones the girl had indicated. I could hear voices in one of the front rooms, but could not understand what they said.

"There was no violent dispute, but a steady hum. Then Bronson jerked the door open. If he had stepped into the hall he would have seen me fitting a key into the door before me. But he spoke before he came out.

"'You're acting like a maniac,' he said. 'You know I can get those things some way; I'm not going to threaten you. It isn't necessary. You know me.'

"'It would be no use,' the other man said. 'I tell you, I haven't seen the notes for ten days.'

"'But you will,' Bronson said savagely. 'You're standing in your own way, that's all. If you're holding out expecting me to raise my figure, you're making a mistake. It's my last offer.'

"'I couldn't take it if it was for a million,' said the man inside the room. 'I'd do it, I expect, if I could. The best of us have our price.'

"Bronson slammed the door then, and flung past me down the hall.

"After a couple of minutes I knocked at the door, and a tall man about your size, Mr. Blakeley, opened it. He was very blond, with a smooth face and blue eyes—what I think you would call a handsome man.

"'I beg your pardon for disturbing you,' I said. 'Can you tell me which is Mr. Johnson's room? Mr. Francis Johnson?'

"'I can not say,' he replied civilly. 'I've only been here a few days.'

"I thanked him and left, but I had had a good look at him, and I think I'd know him readily any place."

I sat for a few minutes thinking it over. "But what did he mean by saying he hadn't seen the notes for ten days? And why is Bronson making the overtures?"

"I think he was lying," Hotchkiss reflected. "Bronson hasn't reached his figure."

"It's a big advance, Mr. Hotchkiss, and I appreciate what you have done more than I can tell you," I said. "And now, if you can locate any of my property in this fellow's room, we'll send him up for larceny, and at least have him where we can get at him. I'm going to Cresson to-morrow, to try to trace him a little from there. But I'll be back in a couple of days, and we'll begin to gather in these scattered threads."

Hotchkiss rubbed his hands together delightedly.

"That's it," he said. "That's what we want to do, Mr. Blakeley. We'll gather up the threads ourselves; if we let the police in too soon, they'll tangle it up again. I'm not vindictive by nature; but when a fellow like Sullivan not only commits a murder, but goes to all sorts of trouble to put the burden of guilt on an innocent man—I say hunt him down, sir!"

"You are convinced, of course, that Sullivan did it?"

"Who else?" He looked over his glasses at me with the air of a man whose mental attitude is unassailable. "Well, listen to this," I said.

Then I told him at length of my encounter with Bronson in the restaurant, of the bargain proposed by Mrs. Conway, and finally of McKnight's new theory. But, although he was impressed, he was far from convinced.

"It's a very vivid piece of imagination," he said drily; "but while it fits the evidence as far as it goes, it doesn't go far enough. How about the stains in lower seven, the dirk, and the wallet? Haven't we even got motive in that telegram from Bronson?"

"Yes," I admitted, "but that bit of chain—"

"Pooh," he said shortly. "Perhaps, like yourself, Sullivan wore glasses with a chain. Our not finding them does not prove they did not exist."

And there I made an error; half confidences are always mistakes. I could not tell of the broken chain in Alison West's gold purse.

It was one o'clock when Hotchkiss finally left. We had by that time arranged a definite course of action—Hotchkiss to search Sullivan's rooms and if possible find evidence to have him held for larceny, while I went to Cresson.

Strangely enough, however, when I entered the train the following morning, Hotchkiss was already there. He had bought a new note-book, and was sharpening a fresh pencil.

"I changed my plans, you see," he said, bustling his newspaper aside for me. "It is no discredit to your intelligence, Mr. Blakeley, but you lack the professional eye, the analytical mind. You legal gentlemen call a spade a spade, although it may be a shovel."

"'A primrose by the river's brim

A yellow primrose was to him,

And nothing more!'"

I quoted as the train pulled out.

Chapter 23

A NIGHT AT THE LAURELS

I slept most of the way to Cresson, to the disgust of the little detective. Finally he struck up an acquaintance with a kindly-faced old priest on his way home to his convent school, armed with a roll of dance music and surreptitious bundles that looked like boxes of candy. From scraps of conversation I gleaned that there had been mysterious occurrences at the convent,—ending in the theft of what the reverend father called vaguely, "a quantity of undermuslins." I dropped asleep at that point, and when I roused a few moments later, the conversation had progressed. Hotchkiss had a diagram on an envelope.

"With this window bolted, and that one inaccessible, and if, as you say, the—er—garments were in a tub here at X, then, as you hold the key to the other door,—I think you said the convent dog did not raise any disturbance? Pardon a personal question, but do you ever walk in your sleep?"

The priest looked bewildered.

"I'll tell you what to do," Hotchkiss said cheerfully, leaning forward, "look around a little yourself before you call in the police. Somnambulism is a queer thing. It's a question whether we are most ourselves sleeping or waking. Ever think of that? Live a saintly life all day, prayers and matins and all that, and the subconscious mind hikes you out of bed at night to steal undermuslins! Subliminal theft, so to speak. Better examine the roof."

I dozed again. When I wakened Hotchkiss sat alone, and the priest, from a corner, was staring at him dazedly, over his breviary.

It was raining when we reached Cresson, a wind-driven rain that had forced the agent at the newsstand to close himself in, and that beat back from the rails in parallel lines of white spray. As he went up the main street, Hotchkiss was cheerfully oblivious of the weather, of the threatening dusk, of our generally draggled condition. My draggled condition, I should say, for he improved every moment,—his eyes brighter, his ruddy face ruddier, his collar newer and glossier. Sometime, when it does not encircle the little man's neck, I shall test that collar with a match.

I was growing steadily more depressed: I loathed my errand and its necessity. I had always held that a man who played the spy on a woman was beneath contempt. Then, I admit I was afraid of what I might learn. For a time, however, this promised to be a negligible quantity. The streets of the straggling little mountain town had been clean-washed of humanity by the downpour. Windows and doors were inhospitably shut, and from around an occasional drawn shade came narrow strips of light that merely emphasized our gloom. When Hotchkiss' umbrella turned inside out, I stopped.

"I don't know where you are going," I snarled, "I don't care. But I'm going to get under cover inside of ten seconds. I'm not amphibious."

I ducked into the next shelter, which happened to be the yawning entrance to a livery stable, and shook myself, dog fashion. Hotchkiss wiped his collar with his handkerchief. It emerged gleaming and unwilted.

"This will do as well as any place," he said, raising his voice above the rattle of the rain. "Got to make a beginning."

I sat down on the usual chair without a back, just inside the door, and stared out at the darkening street. The whole affair had an air of unreality. Now that I was there, I doubted the necessity, or the value, of the journey. I was wet and uncomfortable. Around me, with Cresson as a center, stretched an irregular circumference of mountain, with possibly a ten-mile radius, and in it I was to find the residence of a woman whose first name I did not know, and a man who, so far, had been a purely chimerical person.

Hotchkiss had penetrated the steaming interior of the cave, and now his voice, punctuated by the occasional thud of horses' hoofs, came to me.

"Something light will do," he was saying. "A runabout, perhaps." He came forward rubbing his hands, followed by a thin man in overalls. "Mr. Peck says," he began,—"this is Mr. Peck of Peck and Peck,—says that the place we are looking for is about seven miles from the town. It's clearing, isn't it?"

"It is not," I returned savagely. "And we don't want a runabout, Mr. Peck. What we require is hermetically sealed diving suit. I suppose there isn't a machine to be had?" Mr. Peck gazed at me, in silence: machine to him meant other things than motors. "Automobile," I supplemented. His face cleared.

"None but private affairs. I can give you a good buggy with a rubber apron. Mike, is the doctor's horse in?"

I am still uncertain as to whether the raw-boned roan we took out that night over the mountains was the doctor's horse or not. If it was, the doctor may be a good doctor, but he doesn't know anything about a horse. And furthermore, I hope he didn't need the beast that miserable evening.

While they harnessed the horse, Hotchkiss told me what he had learned.

"Six Curtises in the town and vicinity," he said. "Sort of family name around here. One of them is telegraph operator at the station. Person we are looking for is—was—a wealthy widow with a brother named Sullivan! Both supposed to have been killed on the Flier."

"Her brother," I repeated stupidly.

"You see," Hotchkiss went on, "three people, in one party, took the train here that night, Miss West, Mrs. Curtis and Sullivan. The two women had the drawing-room, Sullivan had lower seven. What we want to find out is just who these people were, where they came from, if Bronson knew them, and how Miss West became entangled with them. She may have married Sullivan, for one thing."

I fell into gloom after that. The roan was led unwillingly into the weather, Hotchkiss and I in eclipse behind the blanket. The liveryman stood in the doorway and called directions to us. "You can't miss it," he finished. "Got the name over the gate anyhow, 'The Laurels.' The servants are still there: leastways, we didn't bring them down." He even took a step into the rain as Hotchkiss picked up the lines. "If you're going to settle the estate," he bawled, "don't forget us, Peck and Peck. A half-bushel of name and a bushel of service."

Hotchkiss could not drive. Born a clerk, he guided the roan much as he would drive a bad pen. And the roan spattered through puddles and splashed ink—mud, that is—until I was in a frenzy of irritation.

"What are we going to say when we get there?" I asked after I had finally taken the reins in my one useful hand. "Get out there at midnight and tell the servants we have come to ask a few questions about the family? It's an idiotic trip anyhow; I wish I had stayed at home."

The roan fell just then, and we had to crawl out and help him up. By the time we had partly unharnessed him our matches were gone, and the small bicycle lamp on the buggy was wavering only too certainly. We were covered with mud, panting with exertion, and even Hotchkiss showed a disposition to be surly. The rain, which had lessened for a time, came on again, the lightning flashes doing more than anything else to reveal our isolated position.

Another mile saw us, if possible, more despondent. The water in our clothes had had time to penetrate: the roan had sprained his shoulder, and drew us along in a series of convulsive jerks. And then through the rain-spattered window of the blanket, I saw a light. It was a small light, rather yellow, and it lasted perhaps thirty seconds. Hotchkiss missed it, and was inclined to doubt me. But in a couple of minutes the roan hobbled to the side of the road and stopped, and I made out a break in the pines and an arched gate.

It was a small gate, too narrow for the buggy. I pulled the horse into as much shelter as possible under the trees, and we got out. Hotchkiss tied the beast and we left him there, head down against the driving rain, drooping and dejected. Then we went toward the house.

It was a long walk. The path bent and twisted, and now and then we lost it. We were climbing as we went. Oddly there were no lights ahead, although it was only ten o'clock,—not later. Hotchkiss kept a little ahead of me, knocking into trees now and then, but finding the path in half the time I should have taken. Once, as I felt my way around a tree in the blackness, I put my hand unexpectedly on his shoulder, and felt a shudder go down my back.

"What do you expect me to do?" he protested, when I remonstrated. "Hang out a red lantern? What was that? Listen."

We both stood peering into the gloom. The sharp patter of the rain on leaves had ceased, and from just ahead there came back to us the stealthy padding of feet in wet soil. My hand closed on Hotchkiss' shoulder, and we listened together, warily. The steps were close by, unmistakable. The next flash of lightning showed nothing moving: the house was in full view now, dark and uninviting, looming huge above a terrace, with an Italian garden at the side. Then the blackness again. Somebody's teeth were chattering: I accused Hotchkiss but he denied it.

"Although I'm not very comfortable, I'll admit," he confessed; "there was something breathing right at my elbow here a moment ago."

"Nonsense!" I took his elbow and steered him in what I made out to be the direction of the steps of the Italian garden. "I saw a deer just ahead by the last flash; that's what you heard. By Jove, I hear wheels."

We paused to listen and Hotchkiss put his hand on something close to us. "Here's your deer," he said. "Bronze."

As we neared the house the sense of surveillance we had had in the park gradually left us. Stumbling over flower beds, running afoul of a sun-dial, groping our way savagely along hedges and thorny banks, we reached the steps finally and climbed the terrace.

It was then that Hotchkiss fell over one of the two stone urns which, with tall boxwood trees in them, mounted guard at each side of the door. He didn't make any attempt to get up. He sat in a puddle on the brick floor of the terrace and clutched his leg and swore softly in Government English.

The occasional relief of the lightning was gone. I could not see an outline of the house before me. We had no matches, and an instant's investigation showed that the windows were boarded and the house closed. Hotchkiss, still recumbent, was ascertaining the damage, tenderly peeling down his stocking.

"Upon my soul," he said finally, "I don't know whether this moisture is blood or rain. I think I've broken a bone."

"Blood is thicker than water," I suggested. "Is it sticky? See if you can move your toes."

There was a pause: Hotchkiss moved his toes. By that time I had found a knocker and was making the night hideous. But there was no response save the wind that blew sodden leaves derisively in our faces. Once Hotchkiss declared he heard a window-sash lifted, but renewed violence with the knocker produced no effect.

"There's only one thing to do," I said finally. "I'll go back and try to bring the buggy up for you. You can't walk, can you?"

Hotchkiss sat back in his puddle and said he didn't think he could stir, but for me to go back to town and leave him, that he didn't have any family dependent on him, and that if he was going to have pneumonia he had probably got it already. I left him there, and started back to get the horse.

If possible, it was worse than before. There was no lightning, and only by a miracle did I find the little gate again. I drew a long breath of relief, followed by another, equally long, of dismay. For I had found the hitching strap and there was nothing at the end of it! In a lull of the wind I seemed to hear, far off, the eager thud of stable-bound feet. So for the second time I climbed the slope to the Laurels, and on the way I thought of many things to say.

I struck the house at a new angle, for I found a veranda, destitute of chairs and furnishings, but dry and evidently roofed. It was better than the terrace, and so, by groping along the wall, I tried to make my way to Hotchkiss. That was how I found the open window. I had passed perhaps six, all closed, and to have my hand grope for the next one, and to find instead the soft drapery of an inner curtain, was startling, to say the least.

I found Hotchkiss at last around an angle of the stone wall, and told him that the horse was gone. He was disconcerted, but not abased; maintaining that it was a new kind of knot that couldn't slip and that the horse must have chewed the halter through! He was less enthusiastic than I had expected about the window.

"It looks uncommonly like a trap," he said. "I tell you there was some one in the park below when we were coming up. Man has a sixth sense that scientists ignore—a sense of the nearness of things. And all the time you have been gone, some one has been watching me."

"Couldn't see you," I maintained; "I can't see you now. And your sense of contiguity didn't tell you about that flower crock."

In the end, of course, he consented to go with me. He was very lame, and I helped him around to the open window. He was full of moral courage, the little man: it was only the physical in him that quailed. And as we groped along, he insisted on going through the window first.

"If it is a trap," he whispered, "I have two arms to your one, and, besides, as I said before, life holds much for you. As for me, the government would merely lose an indifferent employee."

When he found I was going first he was rather hurt, but I did not wait for his protests. I swung my feet over the sill and dropped. I made a clutch at the window-frame with my good hand when I found no floor under my feet, but I was too late. I dropped probably ten feet and landed with a crash that seemed to split my ear-drums. I was thoroughly shaken, but in some miraculous way the bandaged arm had escaped injury.

"For Heaven's sake," Hotchkiss was calling from above, "have you broken your back?"

"No," I returned, as steadily as I could, "merely driven it up through my skull. This is a staircase. I'm coming up to open another window."

It was eerie work, but I accomplished it finally, discovering, not without mishap, a room filled with more tables than I had ever dreamed of, tables that seemed to waylay and strike at me. When I had got a window open, Hotchkiss crawled through, and we were at last under shelter.

Our first thought was for a light. The same laborious investigation that had landed us where we were, revealed that the house was lighted by electricity, and that the plant was not in operation. By accident I stumbled across a tabouret with smoking materials, and found a half dozen matches. The first one showed us the magnitude of the room we stood in, and revealed also a brass candle-stick by the open fireplace, a candle-stick almost four feet high, supporting a candle of similar colossal proportions. It was Hotchkiss who discovered that it had been recently lighted. He held the match to it and peered at it over his glasses.

"Within ten minutes," he announced impressively, "this candle has been burning. Look at the wax! And the wick! Both soft."

"Perhaps it's the damp weather," I ventured, moving a little nearer to the circle of light. A gust of wind came in just then, and the flame turned over on its side and threatened demise. There was something almost ridiculous in the haste with which we put down the window and nursed the flicker to life.

The peculiarly ghost-like appearance of the room added to the uncanniness of the situation. The furniture was swathed in white covers for the winter; even the pictures wore shrouds. And in a niche between two windows a bust on a pedestal, similarly wrapped, one arm extended under its winding sheet, made a most life-like ghost, if any ghost can be life-like.

In the light of the candle we surveyed each other, and we were objects for mirth. Hotchkiss was taking off his sodden shoes and preparing to make himself comfortable, while I hung my muddy raincoat over the ghost in the corner. Thus habited, he presented a rakish but distinctly more comfortable appearance.

"When these people built," Hotchkiss said, surveying the huge dimensions of the room, "they must have bought a mountain and built all over it. What a room!"

It seemed to be a living-room, although Hotchkiss remarked that it was much more like a dead one. It was probably fifty feet long and twenty-five feet wide. It was very high, too, with a domed ceiling, and a gallery ran around the entire room, about fifteen feet above the floor. The candle light did not penetrate beyond the dim outlines of the gallery rail, but I fancied the wall there hung with smaller pictures.

Hotchkiss had discovered a fire laid in the enormous fireplace, and in a few minutes we were steaming before a cheerful blaze. Within the radius of its light and heat, we were comfortable again. But the brightness merely emphasized the gloom of the ghostly corners. We talked in subdued tones, and I smoked, a box of Russian cigarettes which I found in a table drawer. We had decided to stay all night, there being nothing else to do. I suggested a game of double-dummy bridge, but did not urge it when my companion asked me if it resembled euchre. Gradually, as the ecclesiastical candle paled in the firelight, we grew drowsy. I drew a divan into the cheerful area, and stretched myself out for sleep. Hotchkiss, who said the pain in his leg made him wakeful, sat wide-eyed by the fire, smoking a pipe.

I have no idea how much time had passed when something threw itself violently on my chest. I roused with a start and leaped to my feet, and a large Angora cat fell with a thump to the floor. The fire was still bright, and there was an odor of scorched leather through the room, from Hotchkiss' shoes. The little detective was sound asleep, his dead pipe in his fingers. The cat sat back on its haunches and wailed.

The curtain at the door into the hallway bellied slowly out into the room and fell again. The cat looked toward it and opened its mouth for another howl. I thrust at it with my foot, but it refused to move. Hotchkiss stirred uneasily, and his pipe clattered to the floor.

The cat was standing at my feet, staring behind me. Apparently it was following with its eyes, an object unseen to me, that moved behind me. The tip of its tail waved threateningly, but when I wheeled I saw nothing.

I took the candle and made a circuit of the room. Behind the curtain that had moved the door was securely closed. The windows were shut and locked, and everywhere the silence was absolute. The cat followed me majestically. I stooped and stroked its head, but it persisted in its uncanny watching of the corners of the room.

When I went back to my divan, after putting a fresh log on the fire, I was reassured. I took the precaution, and smiled at myself for doing it, to put the fire tongs within reach of my hand. But the cat would not let me sleep. After a time I decided that it wanted water, and I started out in search of some, carrying the candle without the stand. I wandered through several rooms, all closed and dismantled, before I found a small lavatory opening off a billiard room. The cat lapped steadily, and I filled a glass to take back with me. The candle flickered in a sickly fashion that threatened to leave me there lost in the wanderings of the many hallways, and from somewhere there came an occasional violent puff of wind. The cat stuck by my feet, with the hair on its back raised menacingly. I don't like cats; there is something psychic about them.

Hotchkiss was still asleep when I got back to the big room. I moved his boots back from the fire, and trimmed the candle. Then, with sleep gone from me, I lay back on my divan and reflected on many things: on my idiocy in coming; on Alison West, and the fact that only a week before she had been a guest in this very house; on Richey and the constraint that had come between us. From that I drifted back to Alison, and to the barrier my comparative poverty would be.

The emptiness, the stillness were oppressive. Once I heard footsteps coming, rhythmical steps that neither hurried nor dragged, and seemed to mount endless staircases without coming any closer. I realized finally that I had not quite turned off the tap, and that the lavatory, which I had circled to reach, must be quite close.

The cat lay by the fire, its nose on its folded paws, content in the warmth and companionship. I watched it idly. Now and then the green wood hissed in the fire, but the cat never batted an eye. Through an unshuttered window the lightning flashed. Suddenly the cat looked up. It lifted its head and stared directly at the gallery above. Then it blinked, and stared again. I was amused. Not until it had got up on its feet, eyes still riveted on the balcony, tail waving at the tip, the hair on its back a bristling brush, did I glance casually over my head.

From among the shadows a face gazed down at me, a face that seemed a fitting tenant of the ghostly room below. I saw it as plainly as I might see my own face in a mirror. While I stared at it with horrified eyes, the apparition faded. The rail was there, the Bokhara rug still swung from it, but the gallery was empty.

The cat threw back its head and wailed.

Chapter 24

HIS WIFE'S FATHER

I jumped up and seized the fire tongs. The cat's wail had roused Hotchkiss, who was wide-awake at once. He took in my offensive attitude, the tongs, the direction of my gaze, and needed nothing more. As he picked up the candle and darted out into the hall, I followed him. He made directly for the staircase, and part way up he turned off to the right through a small door. We were on the gallery itself; below us the fire gleamed cheerfully, the cat was not in sight. There was no sign of my ghostly visitant, but as we stood there the Bokhara rug, without warning, slid over the railing and fell to the floor below.

"Man or woman?" Hotchkiss inquired in his most professional tone.

"Neither—that is, I don't know. I didn't notice anything but the eyes," I muttered. "They were looking a hole in me. If you'd seen that cat you would realize my state of mind. That was a traditional graveyard yowl."

"I don't think you saw anything at all," he lied cheerfully. "You dozed off, and the rest is the natural result of a meal on a buffet car."

Nevertheless, he examined the Bokhara carefully when we went down, and when I finally went to sleep he was reading the only book in sight—Elwell on Bridge. The first rays of daylight were coming mistily into the room when he roused me. He had his finger on his lips, and he whispered sibilantly while I tried to draw on my distorted boots.

"I think we have him," he said triumphantly. "I've been looking around some, and I can tell you this much. Just before we came in through the window last night, another man came. Only—he did not drop, as you did. He swung over to the stair railing, and then down. The rail is scratched. He was long enough ahead of us to go into the dining-room and get a decanter out of the sideboard. He poured out the liquor into a glass, left the decanter there, and took the whisky into the library across the hall. Then—he broke into a desk, using a paper knife for a jimmy."

"Good Lord, Hotchkiss," I exclaimed; "why, it may have been Sullivan himself! Confound your theories—he's getting farther away every minute."

"It was Sullivan," Hotchkiss returned imperturbably. "And he has not gone. His boots are by the library fire."

"He probably had a dozen pairs where he could get them," I scoffed. "And while you and I sat and slept, the very man we want to get our hands on leered at us over that railing."

"Softly, softly, my friend," Hotchkiss said, as I stamped into my other shoe. "I did not say he was gone. Don't jump at conclusions. It is fatal to reasoning. As a matter of fact, he didn't relish a night on the mountains any more than we did. After he had unintentionally frightened you almost into paralysis, what would my gentleman naturally do? Go out in the storm again? Not if I know the Alice-sit-by-the-fire type. He went up-stairs, well up near the roof, locked himself in and went to bed."

"And he is there now?"

"He is there now."

We had no weapons. I am aware that the traditional hero is always armed, and that Hotchkiss as the low comedian should have had a revolver that missed fire. As a fact, we had nothing of the sort. Hotchkiss carried the fire tongs, but my sense of humor was too strong for me; I declined the poker.

"All we want is a little peaceable conversation with him," I demurred. "We can't brain him first and converse with him afterward. And anyhow, while I can't put my finger on the place, I think your theory is weak. If he wouldn't run a hundred miles through fire and water to get away from us, then he is not the man we want."

Hotchkiss, however, was certain. He had found the room and listened outside the door to the sleeper's heavy breathing, and so we climbed past luxurious suites, revealed in the deepening daylight, past long vistas of hall and boudoir. And we were both badly winded when we got there. It was a tower room, reached by narrow stairs, and well above the roof level. Hotchkiss was glowing.

"It is partly good luck, but not all," he panted in a whisper. "If we had persisted in the search last night, he would have taken alarm and fled. Now—we have him. Are you ready?"

He gave a mighty rap at the door with the fire tongs, and stood expectant. Certainly he was right; some one moved within.

"Hello! Hello there!" Hotchkiss bawled. "You might as well come out. We won't hurt you, if you'll come peaceably."

"Tell him we represent the law," I prompted. "That's the customary thing, you know."

But at that moment a bullet came squarely through the door and flattened itself with a sharp pst against the wall of the tower staircase. We ducked unanimously, dropped back out of range, and Hotchkiss retaliated with a spirited bang at the door with the tongs. This brought another bullet. It was a ridiculous situation. Under the circumstances, no doubt, we should have retired, at least until we had armed ourselves, but Hotchkiss had no end of fighting spirit, and as for me, my blood was up.

"Break the lock," I suggested, and Hotchkiss, standing at the side, out of range, retaliated for every bullet by a smashing blow with the tongs. The shots ceased after a half dozen, and the door was giving, slowly. One of us on each side of the door, we were ready for almost any kind of desperate resistance. As it swung open Hotchkiss poised the tongs; I stood, bent forward, my arm drawn back for a blow.

Nothing happened.

There was not a sound. Finally, at the risk of losing an eye which I justly value, I peered around and into the room. There was no desperado there: only a fresh-faced, trembling-lipped servant, sitting on the edge of her bed, with a quilt around her shoulders and the empty revolver at her feet.

We were victorious, but no conquered army ever beat such a retreat as ours down the tower stairs and into the refuge of the living-room. There, with the door closed, sprawled on the divan, I went from one spasm of mirth into another, becoming sane at intervals, and suffering relapse again every time I saw Hotchkiss' disgruntled countenance. He was pacing the room, the tongs still in his hand, his mouth pursed with irritation. Finally he stopped in front of me and compelled my attention.

"When you have finished cackling," he said with dignity, "I wish to justify my position. Do you think the—er—young woman up-stairs put a pair of number eight boots to dry in the library last night? Do you think she poured the whisky out of that decanter?"

"They have been known to do it," I put in, but his eye silenced me.

"Moreover, if she had been the person who peered at you over the gallery railing last night, don't you suppose, with her—er—belligerent disposition, she could have filled you as full of lead as a window weight?"

"I do," I assented. "It wasn't Alice-sit-by-the-fire. I grant you that. Then who was it?"

Hotchkiss felt certain that it had been Sullivan, but I was not so sure. Why would he have crawled like a thief into his own house? If he had crossed the park, as seemed probable, when we did, he had not made any attempt to use the knocker. I gave it up finally, and made an effort to conciliate the young woman in the tower.

We had heard no sound since our spectacular entrance into her room. I was distinctly uncomfortable as, alone this time, I climbed to the tower staircase. Reasoning from before, she would probably throw a chair at me. I stopped at the foot of the staircase and called.

"Hello up there," I said, in as debonair a manner as I could summon. "Good morning. Wie geht es bei ihen?"

No reply.

"Bon jour, mademoiselle," I tried again. This time there was a movement of some sort from above, but nothing fell on me.

"I—we want to apologize for rousing you so—er—unexpectedly this morning," I went on. "The fact is, we wanted to talk to you, and you—you were hard to waken. We are travelers, lost in your mountains, and we crave a breakfast and an audience."

She came to the door then. I could feel that she was investigating the top of my head from above. "Is Mr. Sullivan with you?" she asked. It was the first word from her, and she was not sure of her voice.

"No. We are alone. If you will come down and look at us you will find us two perfectly harmless people, whose horse—curses on him—departed without leave last night and left us at your gate."

She relaxed somewhat then and came down a step or two. "I was afraid I had killed somebody," she said. "The housekeeper left yesterday, and the other maids went with her."

When she saw that I was comparatively young and lacked the earmarks of the highwayman, she was greatly relieved. She was inclined to fight shy of Hotchkiss, however, for some reason. She gave us a breakfast of a sort, for there was little in the house, and afterward we telephoned to the town for a vehicle. While Hotchkiss examined scratches and replaced the Bokhara rug, I engaged Jennie in conversation.

"Can you tell me," I asked, "who is managing the estate since Mrs. Curtis was killed?"

"No one," she returned shortly.

"Has—any member of the family been here since the accident?"

"No, sir. There was only the two, and some think Mr. Sullivan was killed as well as his sister."

"You don't?"

"No," with conviction.

"Why?"

She wheeled on me with quick suspicion.

"Are you a detective?" she demanded.

"No."

"You told him to say you represented the law."

"I am a lawyer. Some of them misrepresent the law, but I—"

She broke in impatiently.

"A sheriff's officer?"

"No. Look here, Jennie; I am all that I should be. You'll have to believe that. And I'm in a bad position through no fault of my own. I want you to answer some questions. If you will help me, I will do what I can for you. Do you live near here?"

Her chin quivered. It was the first sign of weakness she had shown.

"My home is in Pittsburg," she said, "and I haven't enough money to get there. They hadn't paid any wages for two months. They didn't pay anybody."

"Very well," I returned. "I'll send you back to Pittsburg, Pullman included, if you will tell me some things I want to know."

She agreed eagerly. Outside the window Hotchkiss was bending over, examining footprints in the drive.

"Now," I began, "there has been a Miss West staying here?"

"Yes."

"Mr. Sullivan was attentive to her?"

"Yes. She was the granddaughter of a wealthy man in Pittsburg. My aunt has been in his family for twenty years. Mrs. Curtis wanted her brother to marry Miss West."

"Do you think he did marry her?" I could not keep the excitement out of my voice.

"No. There were reasons"—she stopped abruptly.

"Do you know anything of the family? Are they—were they New Yorkers?"

"They came from somewhere in the south. I have heard Mrs. Curtis say her mother was a Cuban. I don't know much about them, but Mr. Sullivan had a wicked temper, though he didn't look it. Folks say big, light-haired people are easy going, but I don't believe it, sir."

"How long was Miss West here?"

"Two weeks."

I hesitated about further questioning. Critical as my position was, I could not pry deeper into Alison West's affairs. If she had got into the hands of adventurers, as Sullivan and his sister appeared to have been, she was safely away from them again. But something of the situation in the car Ontario was forming itself in my mind: the incident at the farmhouse lacked only motive to be complete. Was Sullivan, after all, a rascal or a criminal? Was the murderer Sullivan or Mrs. Conway? The lady or the tiger again.

Jennie was speaking.

"I hope Miss West was not hurt?" she asked. "We liked her, all of us. She was not like Mrs. Curtis."

I wanted to say that she was not like anybody in the world. Instead—"She escaped with some bruises," I said.

She glanced at my arm. "You were on the train?"

"Yes."

She waited for more questions, but none coming, she went to the door. Then she closed it softly and came back.

"Mrs. Curtis is dead? You are sure of it?" she asked.

"She was killed instantly, I believe. The body was not recovered. But I have reasons for believing that Mr. Sullivan is living."

"I knew it," she said. "I—I think he was here the night before last. That is why I went to the tower room. I believe he would kill me if he could." As nearly as her round and comely face could express it, Jennie's expression was tragic at that moment. I made a quick resolution, and acted on it at once.

"You are not entirely frank with me, Jennie," I protested. "And I am going to tell you more than I have. We are talking at cross purposes."

"I was on the wrecked train, in the same car with Mrs. Curtis, Miss West and Mr. Sullivan. During the night there was a crime committed in that car and Mr. Sullivan disappeared. But he left behind him a chain of circumstantial evidence that involved me completely, so that I may, at any time, be arrested."

Apparently she did not comprehend for a moment. Then, as if the meaning of my words had just dawned on her, she looked up and gasped:

"You mean—Mr. Sullivan committed the crime himself?"

"I think he did."

"What was it?"

"It was murder," I said deliberately.

Her hands clenched involuntarily, and she shrank back. "A woman?" She could scarcely form her words.

"No, a man; a Mr. Simon Harrington, of Pittsburg."

Her effort to retain her self-control was pitiful. Then she broke down and cried, her head on the back of a tall chair.

"It was my fault," she said wretchedly, "my fault, I should not have sent them the word."

After a few minutes she grew quiet. She seemed to hesitate over something, and finally determined to say it.

"You will understand better, sir, when I say that I was raised in the Harrington family. Mr. Harrington was Mr. Sullivan's wife's father!"

Chapter 25

AT THE STATION

So it had been the tiger, not the lady! Well, I had held to that theory all through. Jennie suddenly became a valuable person; if necessary she could prove the connection between Sullivan and the murdered man, and show a motive for the crime. I was triumphant when Hotchkiss came in. When the girl had produced a photograph of Mrs. Sullivan, and I had recognized the bronze-haired girl of the train, we were both well satisfied—which goes to prove the ephemeral nature of most human contentments.

Jennie either had nothing more to say, or feared she had said too much. She was evidently uneasy before Hotchkiss. I told her that Mrs. Sullivan was recovering in a Baltimore hospital, but she already knew it, from some source, and merely nodded. She made a few preparations for leaving, while Hotchkiss and I compared notes, and then, with the cat in her arms, she climbed into the trap from the town. I sat with her, and on the way down she told me a little, not much.

"If you see Mrs. Sullivan," she advised, "and she is conscious, she probably thinks that both her husband and her father were killed in the wreck. She will be in a bad way, sir."

"You mean that she—still cares about her husband?"

The cat crawled over on to my knee, and rubbed its bead against my hand invitingly. Jennie stared at the undulating line of the mountain crests, a colossal sun against a blue ocean of sky. "Yes, she cares," she said softly. "Women are made like that. They say they are cats, but Peter there in your lap wouldn't come back and lick your hand if you kicked him. If—if you have to tell her the truth, be as gentle as you can, sir. She has been good to me—that's why I have played the spy here all summer. It's a thankless thing, spying on people."

"It is that," I agreed soberly.

Hotchkiss and I arrived in Washington late that evening, and, rather than arouse the household, I went to the club. I was at the office early the next morning and admitted myself. McKnight rarely appeared before half after ten, and our modest office force some time after nine. I looked over my previous day's mail and waited, with such patience as I possessed, for McKnight. In the interval I called up Mrs. Klopton and announced that I would dine at home that night. What my household subsists on during my numerous absences I have never discovered. Tea, probably, and crackers. Diligent search when I have made a midnight arrival, never reveals anything more substantial. Possibly I imagine it, but the announcement that I am about to make a journey always seems to create a general atmosphere of depression throughout the house, as though Euphemia and Eliza, and Thomas, the stableman, were already subsisting, in imagination, on Mrs. Klopton's meager fare.

So I called her up and announced my arrival. There was something unusual in her tone, as though her throat was tense with indignation. Always shrill, her elderly voice rasped my ear painfully through the receiver.

"I have changed the butcher, Mr. Lawrence," she announced portentously. "The last roast was a pound short, and his mutton-chops—any self-respecting sheep would refuse to acknowledge them."

As I said before, I can always tell from the voice in which Mrs. Klopton conveys the most indifferent matters, if something of real significance has occurred. Also, through long habit, I have learned how quickest to bring her to the point.

"You are pessimistic this morning," I returned. "What's the matter, Mrs. Klopton? You haven't used that tone since Euphemia baked a pie for the iceman. What is it now? Somebody poison the dog?"

She cleared her throat.

"The house has been broken into, Mr. Lawrence," she said. "I have lived in the best families, and never have I stood by and seen what I saw yesterday—every bureau drawer opened, and my—my most sacred belongings—" she choked.

"Did you notify the police?" I asked sharply.

"Police!" she sniffed. "Police! It was the police that did it—two detectives with a search warrant. I—I wouldn't dare tell you over the telephone what one of them said when he found the whisky and rock candy for my cough."

"Did they take anything?" I demanded, every nerve on edge.

"They took the cough medicine," she returned indignantly, "and they said—"

"Confound the cough medicine!" I was frantic. "Did they take anything else? Were they in my dressing-room?"

"Yes. I threatened to sue them, and I told them what you would do when you came back. But they wouldn't listen. They took away that black sealskin bag you brought home from Pittsburg with you!"

I knew then that my hours of freedom were numbered. To have found Sullivan and then, in support of my case against him, to have produced the bag, minus the bit of chain, had been my intention. But the police had the bag, and, beyond knowing something of Sullivan's history, I was practically no nearer his discovery than before. Hotchkiss hoped he had his man in the house off Washington Circle, but on the very night he had seen him Jennie claimed that Sullivan had tried to enter the Laurels. Then—suppose we found Sullivan and proved the satchel and its contents his? Since the police had the bit of chain it might mean involving Alison in the story. I sat down and buried my face in my hands. There was no escape. I figured it out despondingly.

Against me was the evidence of the survivors of the Ontario that I had been accused of the murder at the time. There had been blood-stains on my pillow and a hidden dagger. Into the bargain, in my possession had been found a traveling-bag containing the dead man's pocket-book.

In my favor was McKnight's theory against Mrs. Conway. She had a motive for wishing to secure the notes, she believed I was in lower ten, and she had collapsed at the discovery of the crime in the morning.

Against both of these theories, I accuse a purely chimerical person named Sullivan, who was not seen by any of the survivors—save one, Alison, whom I could not bring into the case. I could find a motive for his murdering his father-in-law, whom he hated, but again—I would have to drag in the girl.

And not one of the theories explained the telegram and the broken necklace.

Outside the office force was arriving. They were comfortably ignorant of my presence, and over the transom floated scraps of dialogue and the stenographer's gurgling laugh. McKnight had a relative, who was reading law with him, in the intervals between calling up the young women of his acquaintance. He came in singing, and the office boy joined in with the uncertainty of voice of fifteen. I smiled grimly. I was too busy with my own troubles to find any joy in opening the door and startling them into silence. I even heard, without resentment, Blobs of the uncertain voice inquire when "Blake" would be back.

I hoped McKnight would arrive before the arrest occurred. There were many things to arrange. But when at last, impatient of his delay, I telephoned, I found he had been gone for more than an hour. Clearly he was not coming directly to the office, and with such resignation as I could muster I paced the floor and waited.

I felt more alone than I have ever felt in my life. "Born an orphan," as Richey said, I had made my own way, carved out myself such success as had been mine. I had built up my house of life on the props of law and order, and now some unknown hand had withdrawn the supports, and I stood among ruins.

I suppose it is the maternal in a woman that makes a man turn to her when everything else fails. The eternal boy in him goes to have his wounded pride bandaged, his tattered self-respect repaired. If he loves the woman, he wants her to kiss the hurt.

The longing to see Alison, always with me, was stronger than I was that morning. It might be that I would not see her again. I had nothing to say to her save one thing, and that, under the cloud that hung over me, I did not dare to say. But I wanted to see her, to touch her hand—as only a lonely man can crave it, I wanted the comfort of her, the peace that lay in her presence. And so, with every step outside the door a threat, I telephoned to her.

She was gone! The disappointment was great, for my need was great. In a fury of revolt against the scheme of things, I heard that she had started home to Richmond—but that she might still be caught at the station.

To see her had by that time become an obsession. I picked up my hat, threw open the door, and, oblivious of the shock to the office force of my presence, followed so immediately by my exit, I dashed out to the elevator. As I went down in one cage I caught a glimpse of Johnson and two other men going up in the next. I hardly gave them a thought. There was no hansom in sight, and I jumped on a passing car. Let come what might, arrest, prison, disgrace, I was going to see Alison.

I saw her. I flung into the station, saw that it was empty—empty, for she was not there. Then I hurried back to the gates. She was there, a familiar figure in blue, the very gown in which I always thought of her, the one she had worn when, Heaven help me—I had kissed her, at the Carter farm. And she was not alone. Bending over her, talking earnestly, with all his boyish heart in his face, was Richey.

They did not see me, and I was glad of it. After all, it had been McKnight's game first. I turned on my heel and made my way blindly out of the station. Before I lost them I turned once and looked toward them, standing apart from the crowd, absorbed in each other. They were the only two people on earth that I cared about, and I left them there together. Then I went back miserably to the office and awaited arrest.

Chapter 26

ON TO RICHMOND

Strangely enough, I was not disturbed that day. McKnight did not appear at all. I sat at my desk and transacted routine business all afternoon, working with feverish energy. Like a man on the verge of a critical illness or a hazardous journey, I cleared up my correspondence, paid bills until I had writer's cramp from signing checks, read over my will, and paid up my life insurance, made to the benefit of an elderly sister of my mother's. I no longer dreaded arrest. After that morning in the station, I felt that anything would be a relief from the tension. I went home with perfect openness, courting the warrant that I knew was waiting, but I was not molested. The delay puzzled me. The early part of the evening was uneventful. I read until late, with occasional lapses, when my book lay at my elbow, and I smoked and thought. Mrs. Klopton closed the house with ostentatious caution, about eleven, and hung around waiting to enlarge on the outrageousness of the police search. I did not encourage her.

"One would think," she concluded pompously, one foot in the hall, "that you were something you oughtn't to be, Mr. Lawrence. They acted as though you had committed a crime."

"I'm not sure that I didn't, Mrs. Klopton," I said wearily. "Somebody did, the general verdict seems to point my way."

She stared at me in speechless indignation. Then she flounced out. She came back once to say that the paper predicted cooler weather, and that she had put a blanket on my bed, but, to her disappointment, I refused to reopen the subject.

At half past eleven McKnight and Hotchkiss came in. Richey has a habit of stopping his car in front of the house and honking until some one comes out. He has a code of signals with the horn, which I never remember. Two long and a short blast mean, I believe, "Send out a box of cigarettes," and six short blasts, which sound like a police call, mean "Can you lend me some money?" To-night I knew something was up, for he got out and rang the door-bell like a Christian.

They came into the library, and Hotchkiss wiped his collar until it gleamed. McKnight was aggressively cheerful.

"Not pinched yet!" he exclaimed. "What do you think of that for luck! You always were a fortunate devil, Lawrence."

"Yes," I assented, with some bitterness, "I hardly know how to contain myself for joy sometimes. I suppose you know"—to Hotchkiss—"that the police were here while we were at Cresson, and that they found the bag that I brought from the wreck?"

"Things are coming to a head," he said thoughtfully "unless a little plan that I have in mind—" he hesitated.

"I hope so; I am pretty nearly desperate," I said doggedly. "I've got a mental toothache, and the sooner it's pulled the better."

"Tut, tut," said McKnight, "think of the disgrace to the firm if its senior member goes up for life, or—" he twisted his handkerchief into a noose, and went through an elaborate pantomime.

"Although jail isn't so bad, anyhow," he finished, "there are fellows that get the habit and keep going back and going back." He looked at his watch, and I fancied his cheerfulness was strained. Hotchkiss was nervously fumbling my book.

"Did you ever read The Purloined Letter, Mr. Blakeley?" he inquired.

"Probably, years ago," I said. "Poe, isn't it?"

He was choked at my indifference. "It is a masterpiece," he said, with enthusiasm. "I re-read it to-day."

"And what happened?"

"Then I inspected the rooms in the house off Washington Circle. I—I made some discoveries, Mr. Blakeley. For one thing, our man there is left-handed." He looked around for our approval. "There was a small cushion on the dresser, and the scarf pins in it had been stuck in with the left hand."

"Somebody may have twisted the cushion," I objected, but he looked hurt, and I desisted.

"There is only one discrepancy," he admitted, "but it troubles me. According to Mrs. Carter, at the farmhouse, our man wore gaudy pajamas, while I found here only the most severely plain night-shirts."

"Any buttons off?" McKnight inquired, looking again at his watch.

"The buttons were there," the amateur detective answered gravely, "but the buttonhole next the top one was torn through."

McKnight winked at me furtively.

"I am convinced of one thing," Hotchkiss went on, clearing his throat, "the papers are not in that room. Either he carries them with him, or he has sold them."

A sound on the street made both my visitors listen sharply. Whatever it was it passed on, however. I was growing curious and the restraint was telling on McKnight. He has no talent for secrecy. In the interval we discussed the strange occurrence at Cresson, which lost nothing by Hotchkiss' dry narration.

"And so," he concluded, "the woman in the Baltimore hospital is the wife of Henry Sullivan and the daughter of the man he murdered. No wonder he collapsed when he heard of the wreck."

"Joy, probably," McKnight put in. "Is that clock right, Lawrence? Never mind, it doesn't matter. By the way, Mrs. Conway dropped in the office yesterday, while you were away."

"What!" I sprang from my chair.

"Sure thing. Said she had heard great things of us, and wanted us to handle her case against the railroad."

"I would like to know what she is driving at," I reflected. "Is she trying to reach me through you?"

Richey's flippancy is often a cloak for deeper feeling. He dropped it now. "Yes," he said, "she's after the notes, of course. And I'll tell you I felt like a poltroon—whatever that may be—when I turned her down. She stood by the door with her face white, and told me contemptuously that I could save you from a murder charge and wouldn't do it. She made me feel like a cur. I was just as guilty as if I could have obliged her. She hinted that there were reasons and she laid my attitude to beastly motives."

"Nonsense," I said, as easily as I could. Hotchkiss had gone to the window. "She was excited. There are no 'reasons,' whatever she means."

Richey put his hand on my shoulder. "We've been together too long to let any 'reasons' or 'unreasons' come between us, old man," he said, not very steadily. Hotchkiss, who had been silent, here came forward in his most impressive manner. He put his hands under his coat-tails and coughed.

"Mr. Blakeley," he began, "by Mr. McKnight's advice we have arranged a little interview here to-night. If all has gone as I planned, Mr. Henry Pinckney Sullivan is by this time under arrest. Within a very few minutes—he will be here."

"I wanted to talk to him before he was locked up," Richey explained. "He's clever enough to be worth knowing, and, besides, I'm not so cocksure of his guilt as our friend the Patch on the Seat of Government. No murderer worthy of the name needs six different motives for the same crime, beginning with robbery, and ending with an unpleasant father-in-law."

We were all silent for a while. McKnight stationed himself at a window, and Hotchkiss paced the floor expectantly. "It's a great day for modern detective methods," he chirruped. "While the police have been guarding houses and standing with their mouths open waiting for clues to fall in and choke them, we have pieced together, bit by bit, a fabric—"

The door-bell rang, followed immediately by sounds of footsteps in the hall. McKnight threw the door open, and Hotchkiss, raised on his toes, flung out his arm in a gesture of superb eloquence.

"Behold—your man!" he declaimed.

Through the open doorway came a tall, blond fellow, clad in light gray, wearing tan shoes, and followed closely by an officer.

"I brought him here as you suggested, Mr. McKnight," said the constable.

But McKnight was doubled over the library table in silent convulsions of mirth, and I was almost as bad. Little Hotchkiss stood up, his important attitude finally changing to one of chagrin, while the blond man ceased to look angry, and became sheepish.

It was Stuart, our confidential clerk for the last half dozen years!

McKnight sat up and wiped his eyes.

"Stuart," he said sternly, "there are two very serious things we have learned about you. First, you jab your scarf pins into your cushion with your left hand, which is most reprehensible; second, you wear—er—night-shirts, instead of pajamas. Worse than that, perhaps, we find that one of them has a buttonhole torn out at the neck."

Stuart was bewildered. He looked from McKnight to me, and then at the crestfallen Hotchkiss.

"I haven't any idea what it's all about," he said. "I was arrested as I reached my boarding-house to-night, after the theater, and brought directly here. I told the officer it was a mistake."

Poor Hotchkiss tried bravely to justify the fiasco. "You can not deny," he contended, "that Mr. Andrew Bronson followed you to your rooms last Monday evening."

Stuart looked at us and flushed.

"No, I don't deny it," he said, "but there was nothing criminal about it, on my part, at least. Mr. Bronson has been trying to induce me to secure the forged notes for him. But I did not even know where they were."

"And you were not on the wrecked Washington Flier?" persisted Hotchkiss. But McKnight interfered.

"There is no use trying to put the other man's identity on Stuart, Mr. Hotchkiss," he protested. "He has been our confidential clerk for six years, and has not been away from the office a day for a year. I am afraid that the beautiful fabric we have pieced out of all these scraps is going to be a crazy quilt." His tone was facetious, but I could detect the undercurrent of real disappointment.

I paid the constable for his trouble, and he departed. Stuart, still indignant, left to go back to Washington Circle. He shook hands with McKnight and myself magnanimously, but he hurled a look of utter hatred at Hotchkiss, sunk crestfallen in his chair.

"As far as I can see," said McKnight dryly, "we're exactly as far along as we were the day we met at the Carter place. We're not a step nearer to finding our man."

"We have one thing that may be of value," I suggested. "He is the husband of a bronze-haired woman at Van Kirk's hospital, and it is just possible we may trace him through her. I hope we are not going to lose your valuable co-operation, Mr. Hotchkiss?" I asked.

He roused at that to feeble interest, "I—oh, of course not, if you still care to have me, I—I was wondering about—the man who just went out, Stuart, you say? I—told his landlady to-night that he wouldn't need the room again. I hope she hasn't rented it to somebody else."

We cheered him as best we could, and I suggested that we go to Baltimore the next day and try to find the real Sullivan through his wife. He left sometime after midnight, and Richey and I were alone.

He drew a chair near the lamp and lighted a cigarette, and for a time we were silent. I was in the shadow, and I sat back and watched him. It was not surprising, I thought, that she cared for him: women had always loved him, perhaps because he always loved them. There was no disloyalty in the thought: it was the lad's nature to give and crave affection. Only—I was different. I had never really cared about a girl before, and my life had been singularly loveless. I had fought a lonely battle always. Once before, in college, we had both laid ourselves and our callow devotions at the feet of the same girl. Her name was Dorothy—I had forgotten the rest—but I remembered the sequel. In a spirit of quixotic youth I had relinquished my claim in favor of Richey and had gone cheerfully on my way, elevated by my heroic sacrifice to a somber, white-hot martyrdom. As is often the case, McKnight's first words showed our parallel lines of thought.

"I say, Lollie," he asked, "do you remember Dorothy Browne?" Browne, that was it!

"Dorothy Browne?" I repeated. "Oh—why yes, I recall her now. Why?"

"Nothing," he said. "I was thinking about her. That's all. You remember you were crazy about her, and dropped back because she preferred me."

"I got out," I said with dignity, "because you declared you would shoot yourself if she didn't go with you to something or other!"

"Oh, why yes, I recall now!" he mimicked. He tossed his cigarette in the general direction of the hearth and got up. We were both a little conscious, and he stood with his back to me, fingering a Japanese vase on the mantel.

"I was thinking," he began, turning the vase around, "that, if you feel pretty well again, and—and ready to take hold, that I should like to go away for a week or so. Things are fairly well cleaned up at the office."

"Do you mean—you are going to Richmond?" I asked, after a scarcely perceptible pause. He turned and faced me, with his hands thrust in his pockets.

"No. That's off, Lollie. The Sieberts are going for a week's cruise along the coast. I—the hot weather has played hob with me and the cruise means seven days' breeze and bridge."

I lighted a cigarette and offered him the box, but he refused. He was looking haggard and suddenly tired. I could not think of anything to say, and neither could he, evidently. The matter between us lay too deep for speech.

"How's Candida?" he asked.

"Martin says a month, and she will be all right," I returned, in the same tone. He picked up his hat, but he had something more to say. He blurted it out, finally, half way to the door.

"The Seiberts are not going for a couple of days," he said, "and if you want a day or so off to go down to Richmond yourself—"

"Perhaps I shall," I returned, as indifferently as I could. "Not going yet, are you?"

"Yes. It is late." He drew in his breath as if he had something more to say, but the impulse passed. "Well, good night," he said from the doorway.

"Good night, old man."

The next moment the outer door slammed and I heard the engine of the Cannonball throbbing in the street. Then the quiet settled down around me again, and there in the lamplight I dreamed dreams. I was going to see her.

Suddenly the idea of being shut away, even temporarily, from so great and wonderful a world became intolerable. The possibility of arrest before I could get to Richmond was hideous, the night without end.

I made my escape the next morning through the stable back of the house, and then, by devious dark and winding ways, to the office. There, after a conference with Blobs, whose features fairly jerked with excitement, I double-locked the door of my private office and finished off some imperative work. By ten o'clock I was free, and for the twentieth time I consulted my train schedule. At five minutes after ten, with McKnight not yet in sight, Blobs knocked at the door, the double rap we had agreed upon, and on being admitted slipped in and quietly closed the door behind him. His eyes were glistening with excitement, and a purple dab of typewriter ink gave him a peculiarly villainous and stealthy expression.

"They're here," he said, "two of 'em, and that crazy Stuart wasn't on, and said you were somewhere in the building."

A door slammed outside, followed by steps on the uncarpeted outer office.

"This way," said Blobs, in a husky undertone, and, darting into a lavatory, threw open a door that I had always supposed locked. Thence into a back hall piled high with boxes and past the presses of a bookbindery to the freight elevator.

Greatly to Blobs' disappointment, there was no pursuit. I was exhilarated but out of breath when we emerged into an alleyway, and the sharp daylight shone on Blobs' excited face.

"Great sport, isn't it?" I panted, dropping a dollar into his palm, inked to correspond with his face. "Regular walk-away in the hundred-yard dash."

"Gimme two dollars more and I'll drop 'em down the elevator shaft," he suggested ferociously. I left him there with his blood-thirsty schemes, and started for the station. I had a tendency to look behind me now and then, but I reached the station unnoticed. The afternoon was hot, the train rolled slowly along, stopping to pant at sweltering stations, from whose roofs the heat rose in waves. But I noticed these things objectively, not subjectively, for at the end of the journey was a girl with blue eyes and dark brown hair, hair that could—had I not seen it?—hang loose in bewitching tangles or be twisted into little coils of delight.

Chapter 27

THE SEA, THE SAND, THE STARS

I telephoned as soon as I reached my hotel, and I had not known how much I had hoped from seeing her until I learned that she was out of town. I hung up the receiver, almost dizzy with disappointment, and it was fully five minutes before I thought of calling up again and asking if she was within telephone reach. It seemed she was down on the bay staying with the Samuel Forbeses.

Sammy Forbes! It was a name to conjure with just then. In the old days at college I had rather flouted him, but now I was ready to take him to my heart. I remembered that he had always meant well, anyhow, and that he was explosively generous. I called him up.

"By the fumes of gasoline!" he said, when I told him who I was. "Blakeley, the Fount of Wisdom against Woman! Blakeley, the Great Unkissed! Welcome to our city!"

Whereupon he proceeded to urge me to come down to the Shack, and to say that I was an agreeable surprise, because four times in two hours youths had called up to ask if Alison West was stopping with him, and to suggest that they had a vacant day or two. "Oh—Miss West!" I shouted politely. There was a buzzing on the line. "Is she there?" Sam had no suspicions. Was not I in his mind always the Great Unkissed?—which sounds like the Great Unwashed and is even more of a reproach. He asked me down promptly, as I had hoped, and thrust aside my objections.

"Nonsense," he said. "Bring yourself. The lady that keeps my boarding-house is calling to me to insist. You remember Dorothy, don't you, Dorothy Browne? She says unless you have lost your figure you can wear my clothes all right. All you need here is a bathing suit for daytime and a dinner coat for evening."

"It sounds cool," I temporized. "If you are sure I won't put you out—very well, Sam, since you and your wife are good enough. I have a couple of days free. Give my love to Dorothy until I can do it myself."

Sam met me himself and drove me out to the Shack, which proved to be a substantial house overlooking the water. On the way he confided to me that lots of married men thought they were contented when they were merely resigned, but that it was the only life, and that Sam, Junior, could swim like a duck. Incidentally, he said that Alison was his wife's cousin, their respective grandmothers having, at proper intervals, married the same man, and that Alison would lose her good looks if she was not careful.

"I say she's worried, and I stick to it," he said, as he threw the lines to a groom and prepared to get out. "You know her, and she's the kind of girl you think you can read like a book. But you can't; don't fool yourself. Take a good look at her at dinner, Blake; you won't lose your head like the other fellows—and then tell me what's wrong with her. We're mighty fond of Allie."

He went ponderously up the steps, for Sam had put on weight since I knew him. At the door he turned around. "Do you happen to know the MacLures at Seal Harbor?" he asked irrelevantly, but Mrs. Sam came into the hall just then, both hands out to greet me, and, whatever Forbes had meant to say, he did not pick up the subject again.

"We are having tea in here," Dorothy said gaily, indicating the door behind her. "Tea by courtesy, because I think tea is the only beverage that isn't represented. And then we must dress, for this is hop night at the club."

"Which is as great a misnomer as the tea," Sam put in, ponderously struggling out of his linen driving coat. "It's bridge night, and the only hops are in the beer."

He was still gurgling over this as he took me upstairs. He showed me my room himself, and then began the fruitless search for evening raiment that kept me home that night from the club. For I couldn't wear Sam's clothes. That was clear, after a perspiring seance of a half hour.

"I won't do it, Sam," I said, when I had draped his dress-coat on me toga fashion. "Who am I to have clothing to spare, like this, when many a poor chap hasn't even a cellar door to cover him. I won't do it; I'm selfish, but not that selfish."

"Lord," he said, wiping his face, "how you've kept your figure! I can't wear a belt any more; got to have suspenders."

He reflected over his grievance for some time, sitting on the side of the bed. "You could go as you are," he said finally. "We do it all the time, only to-night happens to be the annual something or other, and—" he trailed off into silence, trying to buckle my belt around him. "A good six inches," he sighed. "I never get into a hansom cab any more that I don't expect to see the horse fly up into the air. Well, Allie isn't going either. She turned down Granger this afternoon, the Annapolis fellow you met on the stairs, pigeon-breasted chap—and she always gets a headache on those occasions."

He got up heavily and went to the door. "Granger is leaving," he said, "I may be able to get his dinner coat for you. How well do you know her?" he asked, with his hand on the knob.

"If you mean Dolly—?"

"Alison."

"Fairly well," I said cautiously. "Not as well as I would like to. I dined with her last week in Washington. And—I knew her before that."

Forbes touched the bell instead of going out, and told the servant who answered to see if Mr. Granger's suitcase had gone. If not, to bring it across the hall. Then he came back to his former position on the bed.

"You see, we feel responsible for Allie—near relation and all that," he began pompously. "And we can't talk to the people here at the house—all the men are in love with her, and all the women are jealous. Then—there's a lot of money, too, or will be."

"Confound the money!" I muttered. "That is—nothing. Razor slipped."

"I can tell you," he went on, "because you don't lose your head over every pretty face—although Allie is more than that, of course. But about a month ago she went away—to Seal Harbor, to visit Janet MacLure. Know her?"

"She came home to Richmond yesterday, and then came down here—Allie, I mean. And yesterday afternoon Dolly had a letter from Janet—something about a second man—and saying she was disappointed not to have had Alison there, that she had promised them a two weeks' visit! What do you make of that? And that isn't the worst. Allie herself wasn't in the room, but there were eight other women, and because Dolly had put belladonna in her eyes the night before to see how she would look, and as a result couldn't see anything nearer than across the room, some one read the letter aloud to her, and the whole story is out. One of the cats told Granger and the boy proposed to Allie to-day, to show her he didn't care a tinker's dam where she had been."

"Good boy!" I said, with enthusiasm. I liked the Granger fellow—since he was out of the running. But Sam was looking at me with suspicion.

"Blake," he said, "if I didn't know you for what you are, I'd say you were interested there yourself."

Being so near her, under the same roof, with even the tie of a dubious secret between us, was making me heady. I pushed Forbes toward the door.

"I interested!" I retorted, holding him by the shoulders. "There isn't a word in your vocabulary to fit my condition. I am an island in a sunlit sea of emotion, Sam, a—an empty place surrounded by longing—a—"

"An empty place surrounded by longing!" he retorted. "You want your dinner, that's what's the matter with you—"

I shut the door on him then. He seemed suddenly sordid. Dinner, I thought! Although, as matter of fact, I made a very fair meal when, Granger's suitcase not having gone, in his coat and some other man's trousers, I was finally fit for the amenities. Alison did not come down to dinner, so it was clear she would not go over to the club-house dance. I pled my injured arm and a ficticious, vaguely located sprain from the wreck, as an excuse for remaining at home. Sam regaled the table with accounts of my distrust of women, my one love affair—with Dorothy; to which I responded, as was expected, that only my failure there had kept me single all these years, and that if Sam should be mysteriously missing during the bathing hour to-morrow, and so on.

And when the endless meal was over, and yards of white veils had been tied over pounds of hair—or is it, too, bought by the yard?—and some eight ensembles with their abject complements had been packed into three automobiles and a trap, I drew a long breath and faced about. I had just then only one object in life—to find Alison, to assure her of my absolute faith and confidence in her, and to offer my help and my poor self, if she would let me, in her service.

She was not easy to find. I searched the lower floor, the verandas and the grounds, circumspectly. Then I ran into a little English girl who turned out to be her maid, and who also was searching. She was concerned because her mistress had had no dinner, and because the tray of food she carried would soon be cold. I took the tray from her, on the glimpse of something white on the shore, and that was how I met the Girl again.

She was sitting on an over-turned boat, her chin in her hands, staring out to sea. The soft tide of the bay lapped almost at her feet, and the draperies of her white gown melted hazily into the sands. She looked like a wraith, a despondent phantom of the sea, although the adjective is redundant. Nobody ever thinks of a cheerful phantom. Strangely enough, considering her evident sadness, she was whistling softly to herself, over and over, some dreary little minor air that sounded like a Bohemian dirge. She glanced up quickly when I made a misstep and my dishes jingled. All considered, the tray was out of the picture: the sea, the misty starlight, the girl, with her beauty—even the sad little whistle that stopped now and then to go bravely on again, as though it fought against the odds of a trembling lip. And then I came, accompanied by a tray of little silver dishes that jingled and an unmistakable odor of broiled chicken!

"Oh!" she said quickly; and then, "Oh! I thought you were Jenkins."

"Timeo Danaos—what's the rest of it?" I asked, tendering my offering. "You didn't have any dinner, you know." I sat down beside her. "See, I'll be the table. What was the old fairy tale? 'Little goat bleat: little table appear!' I'm perfectly willing to be the goat, too."

She was laughing rather tremulously.

"We never do meet like other people, do we?" she asked. "We really ought to shake hands and say how are you."

"I don't want to meet you like other people, and I suppose you always think of me as wearing the other fellow's clothes," I returned meekly. "I'm doing it again: I don't seem to be able to help it. These are Granger's that I have on now."

She threw back her head and laughed again, joyously, this time.

"Oh, it's so ridiculous," she said, "and you have never seen me when I was not eating! It's too prosaic!"

"Which reminds me that the chicken is getting cold, and the ice warm," I suggested. "At the time, I thought there could be no place better than the farmhouse kitchen—but this is. I ordered all this for something I want to say to you—the sea, the sand, the stars."

"How alliterative you are!" she said, trying to be flippant. "You are not to say anything until I have had my supper. Look how the things are spilled around!"

But she ate nothing, after all, and pretty soon I put the tray down in the sand. I said little; there was no hurry. We were together, and time meant nothing against that age-long wash of the sea. The air blew her hair in small damp curls against her face, and little by little the tide retreated, leaving our boat an oasis in a waste of gray sand.

"If seven maids with seven mops swept it for half a year Do you suppose, the walrus said, that they could get it clear?"

she threw at me once when she must have known I was going to speak. I held her hand, and as long as I merely held it she let it lie warm in mine. But when I raised it to my lips, and kissed the soft, open palm, she drew it away without displeasure.

"Not that, please," she protested, and fell to whistling softly again, her chin in her hands. "I can't sing," she said, to break an awkward pause, "and so, when I'm fidgety, or have something on my mind, I whistle. I hope you don't dislike it?"

"I love it," I asserted warmly. I did; when she pursed her lips like that I was mad to kiss them.

"I saw you—at the station," she said, suddenly. "You—you were in a hurry to go." I did not say anything, and after a pause she drew a long breath. "Men are queer, aren't they?" she said, and fell to whistling again.

After a while she sat up as if she had made a resolution. "I am going to confess something," she announced suddenly. "You said, you know, that you had ordered all this for something you—you wanted to say to me. But the fact is, I fixed it all—came here, I mean, because—I knew you would come, and I had something to tell you. It was such a miserable thing I—needed the accessories to help me out."

"I don't want to hear anything that distresses you to tell," I assured her. "I didn't come here to force your confidence, Alison. I came because I couldn't help it." She did not object to my use of her name.

"Have you found—your papers?" she asked, looking directly at me for almost the first time.

"Not yet. We hope to."

"The—police have not interfered with you?"

"They haven't had any opportunity," I equivocated. "You needn't distress yourself about that, anyhow."

"But I do. I wonder why you still believe in me? Nobody else does."

"I wonder," I repeated, "why I do!"

"If you produce Harry Sullivan," she was saying, partly to herself, "and if you could connect him with Mr. Bronson, and get a full account of why he was on the train, and all that, it—it would help, wouldn't it?"

I acknowledged that it would. Now that the whole truth was almost in my possession, I was stricken with the old cowardice. I did not want to know what she might tell me. The yellow line on the horizon, where the moon was coming up, was a broken bit of golden chain: my heel in the sand was again pressed on a woman's yielding fingers: I pulled myself together with a jerk.

"In order that what you might tell me may help me, if it will," I said constrainedly, "it would be necessary, perhaps, that you tell it to the police. Since they have found the end of the necklace—"

"The end of the necklace!" she repeated slowly. "What about the end of the necklace?"

I stared at her. "Don't you remember"—I leaned forward—"the end of the cameo necklace, the part that was broken off, and was found in the black sealskin bag, stained with—with blood?"

"Blood," she said dully. "You mean that you found the broken end? And then—you had my gold pocket-book, and you saw the necklace in it, and you—must have thought—"

"I didn't think anything," I hastened to assure her. "I tell you, Alison, I never thought of anything but that you were unhappy, and that I had no right to help you. God knows, I thought you didn't want me to help you."

She held out her hand to me and I took it between both of mine. No word of love had passed between us, but I felt that she knew and understood. It was one of the moments that come seldom in a lifetime, and then only in great crises, a moment of perfect understanding and trust.

Then she drew her hand away and sat, erect and determined, her fingers laced in her lap. As she talked the moon came up slowly and threw its bright pathway across the water. Back of us, in the trees beyond the sea wall, a sleepy bird chirruped drowsily, and a wave, larger and bolder than its brothers, sped up the sand, bringing the moon's silver to our very feet. I bent toward the girl.

"I am going to ask just one question."

"Anything you like." Her voice was almost dreary. "Was it because of anything you are going to tell me that you refused Richey?"

She drew her breath in sharply.

"No," she said, without looking at me. "No. That was not the reason."

Chapter 28

ALISON'S STORY

She told her story evenly, with her eyes on the water, only now and then, when I, too, sat looking seaward, I thought she glanced at me furtively. And once, in the middle of it, she stopped altogether.

"You don't realize it, probably," she protested, "but you look like a—a war god. Your face is horrible."

"I will turn my back, if it will help any," I said stormily, "but if you expect me to look anything but murderous, why, you don't know what I am going through with. That's all."

The story of her meeting with the Curtis woman was brief enough. They had met in Rome first, where Alison and her mother had taken a villa for a year. Mrs. Curtis had hovered on the ragged edges of society there, pleading the poverty of the south since the war as a reason for not going out more. There was talk of a brother, but Alison had not seen him, and after a scandal which implicated Mrs. Curtis and a young attache of the Austrian embassy, Alison had been forbidden to see the woman.

"The women had never liked her, anyhow," she said. "She did unconventional things, and they are very conventional there. And they said she did not always pay her—her gambling debts. I didn't like them. I thought they didn't like her because she was poor—and popular. Then—we came home, and I almost forgot her, but last spring, when mother was not well—she had taken grandfather to the Riviera, and it always uses her up—we went to Virginia Hot Springs, and we met them there, the brother, too, this time. His name was Sullivan, Harry Pinckney Sullivan."

"I know. Go on."

"Mother had a nurse, and I was alone a great deal, and they were very kind to me. I—I saw a lot of them. The brother rather attracted me, partly—partly because he did not make love to me. He even seemed to avoid me, and I was piqued. I had been spoiled, I suppose. Most of the other men I knew had—had—"

"I know that, too," I said bitterly, and moved away from her a trifle. I was brutal, but the whole story was a long torture. I think she knew what I was suffering, for she showed no resentment.

"It was early and there were few people around—none that I cared about. And mother and the nurse played cribbage eternally, until I felt as though the little pegs were driven into my brain. And when Mrs. Curtis arranged drives and picnics, I—I slipped away and went. I suppose you won't believe me, but I had never done that kind of thing before, and I—well, I have paid up, I think."

"What sort of looking chap was Sullivan?" I demanded. I had got up and was pacing back and forward on the sand. I remember kicking savagely at a bit of water-soaked board that lay in my way.

"Very handsome—as large as you are, but fair, and even more erect."

I drew my shoulders up sharply. I am straight enough, but I was fairly sagging with jealous rage.

"When mother began to get around, somebody told her that I had been going about with Mrs. Curtis and her brother, and we had a dreadful time. I was dragged home like a bad child. Did anybody ever do that to you?"

"Nobody ever cared. I was born an orphan," I said, with a cheerless attempt at levity. "Go on."

"If Mrs. Curtis knew, she never said anything. She wrote me charming letters, and in the summer, when they went to Cresson, she asked me to visit her there. I was too proud to let her know that I could not go where I wished, and so—I sent Polly, my maid, to her aunt's in the country, pretended to go to Seal Harbor, and really went to Cresson. You see I warned you it would be an unpleasant story."

I went over and stood in front of her. All the accumulated jealousy of the last few weeks had been fired by what she told me. If Sullivan had come across the sands just then, I think I would have strangled him with my hands, out of pure hate.

"Did you marry him?" I demanded. My voice sounded hoarse and strange in my ears. "That's all I want to know. Did you marry him?"

"No."

I drew a long breath.

"You—cared about him?"

She hesitated.

"No," she said finally. "I did not care about him."

I sat down on the edge of the boat and mopped my hot face. I was heartily ashamed of myself, and mingled with my abasement was a great relief. If she had not married him, and had not cared for him, nothing else was of any importance.

"I was sorry, of course, the moment the train had started, but I had wired I was coming, and I could not go back, and then when I got there, the place was charming. There were no neighbors, but we fished and rode and motored, and—it was moonlight, like this."

I put my hand over both of hers, clasped in her lap. "I know," I acknowledged repentantly, "and—people do queer things when it is moonlight. The moon has got me to-night, Alison. If I am a boor, remember that, won't you?"

Her fingers lay quiet under mine. "And so," she went on with a little sigh, "I began to think perhaps I cared. But all the time I felt that there was something not quite right. Now and then Mrs. Curtis would say or do something that gave me a queer start, as if she had dropped a mask for a moment. And there was trouble with the servants; they were almost insolent. I couldn't understand. I don't know when it dawned on me that the old Baron Cavalcanti had been right when he said they were not my kind of people. But I wanted to get away, wanted it desperately."

"Of course, they were not your kind," I cried. "The man was married! The girl Jennie, a housemaid, was a spy in Mrs. Sullivan's employ. If he had pretended to marry you I would have killed him! Not only that, but the man he murdered, Harrington, was his wife's father. And I'll see him hang by the neck yet if it takes every energy and every penny I possess."

I could have told her so much more gently, have broken the shock for her; I have never been proud of that evening on the sand. I was alternately a boor and a ruffian—like a hurt youngster who passes the blow that has hurt him on to his playmate, that both may bawl together. And now Alison sat, white and cold, without speech.

"Married!" she said finally, in a small voice. "Why, I don't think it is possible, is it? I—I was on my way to Baltimore to marry him myself, when the wreck came."

"But you said you didn't care for him!" I protested, my heavy masculine mind unable to jump the gaps in her story. And then, without the slightest warning, I realized that she was crying. She shook off my hand and fumbled for her handkerchief, and failing to find it, she accepted the one I thrust into her wet fingers.

Then, little by little, she told me from the handkerchief, a sordid story of a motor trip in the mountains without Mrs. Curtis, of a lost road and a broken car, and a rainy night when they—she and Sullivan, tramped eternally and did not get home. And of Mrs. Curtis, when they got home at dawn, suddenly grown conventional and deeply shocked. Of her own proud, half-disdainful consent to make possible the hackneyed compromising situation by marrying the rascal, and then—of his disappearance from the train. It was so terrible to her, such a Heaven-sent relief to me, in spite of my rage against Sullivan, that I laughed aloud. At which she looked at me over the handkerchief.

"I know it's funny," she said, with a catch in her breath. "When I think that I nearly married a murderer—and didn't—I cry for sheer joy." Then she buried her face and cried again.

"Please don't," I protested unsteadily. "I won't be responsible if you keep on crying like that. I may forget that I have a capital charge hanging over my head, and that I may be arrested at any moment."

That brought her out of the handkerchief at once. "I meant to be so helpful," she said, "and I've thought of nothing but myself! There were some things I meant to tell you. If Jennie was—what you say, then I understand why she came to me just before I left. She had been packing my things and she must have seen what condition I was in, for she came over to me when I was getting my wraps on, to leave, and said, 'Don't do it, Miss West, I beg you won't do it; you'll be sorry ever after.' And just then Mrs. Curtis came in and Jennie slipped out."

"That was all?"

"No. As we went through the station the telegraph operator gave Har—Mr. Sullivan a message. He read it on the platform, and it excited him terribly. He took his sister aside and they talked together. He was white with either fear or anger—I don't know which. Then, when we boarded the train, a woman in black, with beautiful hair, who was standing on the car platform, touched him on the arm and then drew back. He looked at her and glanced away again, but she reeled as if he had struck her."

"Then what?" The situation was growing clearer.

"Mrs. Curtis and I had the drawing-room. I had a dreadful night, just sleeping a little now and then. I dreaded to see dawn come. It was to be my wedding-day. When we found Harry had disappeared in the night, Mrs. Curtis was in a frenzy. Then—I saw his cigarette case in your hand. I had given it to him. You wore his clothes. The murder was discovered and you were accused of it! What could I do? And then, afterward, when I saw him asleep at the farmhouse, I—I was panic-stricken. I locked him in and ran. I didn't know why he did it, but—he had killed a man."

Some one was calling Alison through a megaphone, from the veranda. It sounded like Sam. "All-ee," he called. "All-ee! I'm going to have some anchovies on toast! All-ee!" Neither of us heard.

"I wonder," I reflected, "if you would be willing to repeat a part of that story—just from the telegram on—to a couple of detectives, say on Monday. If you would tell that, and—how the end of your necklace got into the sealskin bag—"

"My necklace!" she repeated. "But it isn't mine. I picked it up in the car."

"All-ee!" Sam again. "I see you down there. I'm making a julep!"

Alison turned and called through her hands. "Coming in a moment, Sam," she said, and rose. "It must be very late: Sam is home. We would better go back to the house."

"Don't," I begged her. "Anchovies and juleps and Sam will go on for ever, and I have you such a little time. I suppose I am only one of a dozen or so, but—you are the only girl in the world. You know I love you, don't you, dear?"

Sam was whistling, an irritating bird call, over and over. She pursed her red lips and answered him in kind. It was more than I could endure.

"Sam or no Sam," I said firmly, "I am going to kiss you!"

But Sam's voice came strident through the megaphone. "Be good, you two," he bellowed, "I've got the binoculars!" And so, under fire, we walked sedately back to the house. My pulses were throbbing—the little swish of her dress beside me on the grass was pain and ecstasy. I had but to put out my hand to touch her, and I dared not.

Sam, armed with a megaphone and field glasses, bent over the rail and watched us with gleeful malignity.

"Home early, aren't you?" Alison called, when we reached the steps.

"Led a club when my partner had doubled no-trumps, and she fainted. Damn the heart convention!" he said cheerfully. "The others are not here yet."

Three hours later I went up to bed. I had not seen Alison alone again. The noise was at its height below, and I glanced down into the garden, still bright in the moonlight. Leaning against a tree, and staring interestedly into the billiard room, was Johnson.

Chapter 29

IN THE DINING-ROOM

That was Saturday night, two weeks after the wreck. The previous five days had been full of swift-following events—the woman in the house next door, the picture in the theater of a man about to leap from the doomed train, the dinner at the Dallases', and Richey's discovery that Alison was the girl in the case. In quick succession had come our visit to the Carter place, the finding of the rest of the telegram, my seeing Alison there, and the strange interview with Mrs. Conway. The Cresson trip stood out in my memory for its serio-comic horrors and its one real thrill. Then—the discovery by the police of the seal-skin bag and the bit of chain; Hotchkiss producing triumphantly Stuart for Sullivan and his subsequent discomfiture; McKnight at the station with Alison, and later the confession that he was out of the running.

And yet, when I thought it all over, the entire week and its events were two sides of a triangle that was narrowing rapidly to an apex, a point. And the said apex was at that moment in the drive below my window, resting his long legs by sitting on a carriage block, and smoking a pipe that made the night hideous. The sense of the ridiculous is very close to the sense of tragedy. I opened my screen and whistled, and Johnson looked up and grinned. We said nothing. I held up a handful of cigars, he extended his hat, and when I finally went to sleep, it was to a soothing breeze that wafted in salt air and a faint aroma of good tobacco. I was thoroughly tired, but I slept restlessly, dreaming of two detectives with Pittsburg warrants being held up by Hotchkiss at the point of a splint, while Alison fastened their hands with a chain that was broken and much too short. I was roused about dawn by a light rap at the door, and, opening it, I found Forbes, in a pair of trousers and a pajama coat. He was as pleasant as most fleshy people are when they have to get up at night, and he said the telephone had been ringing for an hour, and he didn't know why somebody else in the blankety-blank house couldn't have heard it. He wouldn't get to sleep until noon.

As he was palpably asleep on his feet, I left him grumbling and went to the telephone. It proved to be Richey, who had found me by the simple expedient of tracing Alison, and he was jubilant.

"You'll have to come back," he said. "Got a railroad schedule there?"

"I don't sleep with one in my pocket," I retorted, "but if you'll hold the line I'll call out the window to Johnson. He's probably got one.'"

"Johnson!" I could hear the laugh with which McKnight comprehended the situation. He was still chuckling when I came back.

"Train to Richmond at six-thirty A.M.," I said. "What time is it now?"

"Four. Listen, Lollie. We've got him. Do you hear? Through the woman at Baltimore. Then the other woman, the lady of the restaurant"—he was obviously avoiding names—"she is playing our cards for us. No—I don't know why, and I don't care. But you be at the Incubator to-night at eight o'clock. If you can't shake Johnson, bring him, bless him."

To this day I believe the Sam Forbeses have not recovered from the surprise of my unexpected arrival, my one appearance at dinner in Granger's clothes, and the note on my dresser which informed them the next morning that I had folded my tents like the Arabs and silently stole away. For at half after five Johnson and I, the former as uninquisitive as ever, were on our way through the dust to the station, three miles away, and by four that afternoon we were in Washington. The journey had been uneventful. Johnson relaxed under the influence of my tobacco, and spoke at some length on the latest improvements in gallows, dilating on the absurdity of cutting out the former free passes to see the affair in operation. I remember, too, that he mentioned the curious anomaly that permits a man about to be hanged to eat a hearty meal. I did not enjoy my dinner that night.

Before we got into Washington I had made an arrangement with Johnson to surrender myself at two the following afternoon. Also, I had wired to Alison, asking her if she would carry out the contract she had made. The detective saw me home, and left me there. Mrs. Klopton received me with dignified reserve. The very tone in which she asked me when I would dine told me that something was wrong.

"Now—what is it, Mrs. Klopton?" I demanded finally, when she had informed me, in a patient and long-suffering tone, that she felt worn out and thought she needed a rest.

"When I lived with Mr. Justice Springer," she began acidly, her mending-basket in her hands, "it was an orderly, well-conducted household. You can ask any of the neighbors. Meals were cooked and, what's more, they were eaten; there was none of this 'here one day and gone the next' business."

"Nonsense," I observed. "You're tired, that's all, Mrs. Klopton. And I wish you would go out; I want to bathe."

"That's not all," she said with dignity, from the doorway. "Women coming and going here, women whose shoes I am not fit—I mean, women who are not fit to touch my shoes—coming here as insolent as you please, and asking for you."

"Good heavens!" I exclaimed. "What did you tell them—her, whichever it was?"

"Told her you were sick in a hospital and wouldn't be out for a year!" she said triumphantly. "And when she said she thought she'd come in and wait for you, I slammed the door on her."

"What time was she here?"

"Late last night. And she had a light-haired man across the street. If she thought I didn't see him, she don't know me." Then she closed the door and left me to my bath and my reflections.

At five minutes before eight I was at the Incubator, where I found Hotchkiss and McKnight. They were bending over a table, on which lay McKnight's total armament—a pair of pistols, an elephant gun and an old cavalry saber.

"Draw up a chair and help yourself to pie," he said, pointing to the arsenal. "This is for the benefit of our friend Hotchkiss here, who says he is a small man and fond of life."

Hotchkiss, who had been trying to get the wrong end of a cartridge into the barrel of one of the revolvers, straightened himself and mopped his face.

"We have desperate people to handle," he said pompously, "and we may need desperate means."

"Hotchkiss is like the small boy whose one ambition was to have people grow ashen and tremble at the mention of his name," McKnight jibed. But they were serious enough, both of them, under it all, and when they had told me what they planned, I was serious, too.

"You're compounding a felony," I remonstrated, when they had explained. "I'm not eager to be locked away, but, by Jove, to offer her the stolen notes in exchange for Sullivan!"

"We haven't got either of them, you know," McKnight remonstrated, "and we won't have, if we don't start. Come along, Fido," to Hotchkiss.

The plan was simplicity itself. According to Hotchkiss, Sullivan was to meet Bronson at Mrs. Conway's apartment, at eight-thirty that night, with the notes. He was to be paid there and the papers destroyed. "But just before that interesting finale," McKnight ended, "we will walk in, take the notes, grab Sullivan, and give the police a jolt that will put them out of the count."

I suppose not one of us, slewing around corners in the machine that night, had the faintest doubt that we were on the right track, or that Fate, scurvy enough before, was playing into our hands at last. Little Hotchkiss was in a state of fever; he alternately twitched and examined the revolver, and a fear that the two movements might be synchronous kept me uneasy. He produced and dilated on the scrap of pillow slip from the wreck, and showed me the stiletto, with its point in cotton batting for safekeeping. And in the intervals he implored Richey not to make such fine calculations at the corners.

We were all grave enough and very quiet, however, when we reached the large building where Mrs. Conway had her apartment. McKnight left the power on, in case we might want to make a quick get-away, and Hotchkiss gave a final look at the revolver. I had no weapon. Somehow it all seemed melodramatic to the verge of farce. In the doorway Hotchkiss was a half dozen feet ahead; Richey fell back beside me. He dropped his affectation of gayety, and I thought he looked tired. "Same old Sam, I suppose?" he asked.

"Same, only more of him."

"I suppose Alison was there? How is she?" he inquired irrelevantly.

"Very well. I did not see her this morning."

Hotchkiss was waiting near the elevator. McKnight put his hand on my arm. "Now, look here, old man," he said, "I've got two arms and a revolver, and you've got one arm and a splint. If Hotchkiss is right, and there is a row, you crawl under a table."

"The deuce I will!" I declared scornfully.

We crowded out of the elevator at the fourth floor, and found ourselves in a rather theatrical hallway of draperies and armor. It was very quiet; we stood uncertainly after the car had gone, and looked at the two or three doors in sight. They were heavy, covered with metal, and sound proof. From somewhere above came the metallic accuracy of a player-piano, and through the open window we could hear—or feel—the throb of the Cannonball's engine.

"Well, Sherlock," McKnight said, "what's the next move in the game? Is it our jump, or theirs? You brought us here."

None of us knew just what to do next. No sound of conversation penetrated the heavy doors. We waited uneasily for some minutes, and Hotchkiss looked at his watch. Then he put it to his ear.

"Good gracious!" he exclaimed, his head cocked on one side, "I believe it has stopped. I'm afraid we are late."

We were late. My watch and Hotchkiss' agreed at nine o clock, and, with the discovery that our man might have come and gone, our zest in the adventure began to flag. McKnight motioned us away from the door and rang the bell. There was no response, no sound within. He rang it twice, the last time long and vigorously, without result. Then he turned and looked at us.

"I don't half like this," he said. "That woman is in; you heard me ask the elevator boy. For two cents I'd—"

I had seen it when he did. The door was ajar about an inch, and a narrow wedge of rose-colored light showed beyond. I pushed the door a little and listened. Then, with both men at my heels, I stepped into the private corridor of the apartment and looked around. It was a square reception hall, with rugs on the floor, a tall mahogany rack for hats, and a couple of chairs. A lantern of rose-colored glass and a desk light over a writing-table across made the room bright and cheerful. It was empty.

None of us was comfortable. The place was full of feminine trifles that made us feel the weakness of our position. Some such instinct made McKnight suggest division.

"We look like an invading army," he said. "If she's here alone, we will startle her into a spasm. One of us could take a look around and—"

"What was that? Didn't you hear something?"

The sound, whatever it had been, was not repeated. We went awkwardly out into the hall, very uncomfortable, all of us, and flipped a coin. The choice fell to me, which was right enough, for the affair was mine, primarily.

"Wait just inside the door," I directed, "and if Sullivan comes, or anybody that answers his description, grab him without ceremony and ask him questions afterwards."

The apartment, save in the hallway, was unlighted. By one of those freaks of arrangement possible only in the modern flat, I found the kitchen first, and was struck a smart and unexpected blow by a swinging door. I carried a handful of matches, and by the time I had passed through a butler's pantry and a refrigerator room I was completely lost in the darkness. Until then the situation had been merely uncomfortable; suddenly it became grisly. From somewhere near came a long-sustained groan, followed almost instantly by the crash of something—glass or china—on the floor.

I struck a fresh match, and found myself in a narrow rear hallway. Behind me was the door by which I must have come; with a keen desire to get back to the place I had started from, I opened the door and attempted to cross the room. I thought I had kept my sense of direction, but I crashed without warning into what, from the resulting jangle, was the dining-table, probably laid for dinner. I cursed my stupidity in getting into such a situation, and I cursed my nerves for making my hand shake when I tried to strike a match. The groan had not been repeated.

I braced myself against the table and struck the match sharply against the sole of my shoe. It flickered faintly and went out. And then, without the slightest warning, another dish went off the table. It fell with a thousand splinterings; the very air seemed broken into crashing waves of sound. I stood still, braced against the table, holding the red end of the dying match, and listened. I had not long to wait; the groan came again, and I recognized it, the cry of a dog in straits. I breathed again.

"Come, old fellow," I said. "Come on, old man. Let's have a look at you."

I could hear the thud of his tail on the floor, but he did not move. He only whimpered. There is something companionable in the presence of a dog, and I fancied this dog in trouble. Slowly I began to work my way around the table toward him.

"Good boy," I said, as he whimpered. "We'll find the light, which ought to be somewhere or other around here, and then—"

I stumbled over something, and I drew back my foot almost instantly. "Did I step on you, old man?" I exclaimed, and bent to pat him. I remember straightening suddenly and hearing the dog pad softly toward me around the table. I recall even that I had put the matches down and could not find them. Then, with a bursting horror of the room and its contents, of the gibbering dark around me, I turned and made for the door by which I had entered.

I could not find it. I felt along the endless wainscoting, past miles of wall. The dog was beside me, I think, but he was part and parcel now, to my excited mind, with the Thing under the table. And when, after aeons of search, I found a knob and stumbled into the reception hall, I was as nearly in a panic as any man could be.

I was myself again in a second, and by the light from the hall I led the way back to the tragedy I had stumbled on. Bronson still sat at the table, his elbows propped on it, his cigarette still lighted, burning a hole in the cloth. Partly under the table lay Mrs. Conway face down. The dog stood over her and wagged his tail.

McKnight pointed silently to a large copper ashtray, filled with ashes and charred bits of paper.

"The notes, probably," he said ruefully. "He got them after all, and burned them before her. It was more than she could stand. Stabbed him first and then herself."

Hotchkiss got up and took off his hat. "They are dead," he announced solemnly, and took his note-book out of his hatband.

McKnight and I did the only thing we could think of—drove Hotchkiss and the dog out of the room, and closed and locked the door. "It's a matter for the police," McKnight asserted. "I suppose you've got an officer tied to you somewhere, Lawrence? You usually have."

We left Hotchkiss in charge and went down-stairs. It was McKnight who first saw Johnson, leaning against a park railing across the street, and called him over. We told him in a few words what we had found, and he grinned at me cheerfully.

"After while, in a few weeks or months, Mr. Blakeley," he said, "when you get tired of monkeying around with the blood-stain and finger-print specialist up-stairs, you come to me. I've had that fellow you want under surveillance for ten days!"

Chapter 30

FINER DETAILS

At ten minutes before two the following day, Monday, I arrived at my office. I had spent the morning putting my affairs in shape, and in a trip to the stable. The afternoon would see me either a free man or a prisoner for an indefinite length of time, and, in spite of Johnson's promise to produce Sullivan, I was more prepared for the latter than the former.

Blobs was watching for me outside the door, and it was clear that he was in a state of excitement bordering on delirium. He did nothing, however, save to tip me a wink that meant "As man to man, I'm for you." I was too much engrossed either to reprove him or return the courtesy, but I heard him follow me down the hall to the small room where we keep outgrown lawbooks, typewriter supplies and, incidentally, our wraps. I was wondering vaguely if I would ever hang my hat on its nail again, when the door closed behind me. It shut firmly, without any particular amount of sound, and I was left in the dark. I groped my way to it, irritably, to find it locked on the outside. I shook it frantically, and was rewarded by a sibilant whisper through the keyhole.

"Keep quiet," Blobs was saying huskily. "You're in deadly peril. The police are waiting in your office, three of 'em. I'm goin' to lock the whole bunch in and throw the key out of the window."

"Come back here, you imp of Satan!" I called furiously, but I could hear him speeding down the corridor, and the slam of the outer office door by which he always announced his presence. And so I stood there in that ridiculous cupboard, hot with the heat of a steaming September day, musty with the smell of old leather bindings, littered with broken overshoes and handleless umbrellas. I was apoplectic with rage one minute, and choked with laughter the next. It seemed an hour before Blobs came back.

He came without haste, strutting with new dignity, and paused outside my prison door.

"Well, I guess that will hold them for a while," he remarked comfortably, and proceeded to turn the key. "I've got 'em fastened up like sardines in a can!" he explained, working with the lock. "Gee whiz! you'd ought to hear 'em!" When he got his breath after the shaking I gave him, he began to splutter. "How'd I know?" he demanded sulkily. "You nearly broke your neck gettin' away the other time. And I haven't got the old key. It's lost."

"Where's it lost?" I demanded, with another gesture toward his coat collar.

"Down the elevator shaft." There was a gleam of indignant satisfaction through his tears of rage and humiliation.

And so, while he hunted the key in the debris at the bottom of the shaft, I quieted his prisoners with the assurance that the lock had slipped, and that they would be free as lords as soon as we could find the janitor with a pass-key. Stuart went down finally and discovered Blobs, with the key in his pocket, telling the engineer how he had tried to save me from arrest and failed. When Stuart came up he was almost cheerful, but Blobs did not appear again that day.

Simultaneous with the finding of the key came Hotchkiss, and we went in together. I shook hands with two men who, with Hotchkiss, made a not very animated group. The taller one, an oldish man, lean and hard, announced his errand at once.

"A Pittsburg warrant?" I inquired, unlocking my cigar drawer.

"Yes. Allegheny County has assumed jurisdiction, the exact locality where the crime was committed being in doubt." He seemed to be the spokesman. The other, shorter and rotund, kept an amiable silence. "We hope you will see the wisdom of waiving extradition," he went on. "It will save time."

"I'll come, of course," I agreed. "The sooner the better. But I want you to give me an hour here, gentlemen. I think we can interest you. Have a cigar?"

The lean man took a cigar; the rotund man took three, putting two in his pocket.

"How about the catch of that door?" he inquired jovially. "Any danger of it going off again?" Really, considering the circumstances, they were remarkably cheerful. Hotchkiss, however, was not. He paced the floor uneasily, his hands under his coat-tails. The arrival of McKnight created a diversion; he carried a long package and a corkscrew, and shook hands with the police and opened the bottle with a single gesture.

"I always want something to cheer on these occasions," he said. "Where's the water, Blakeley? Everybody ready?" Then in French he toasted the two detectives.

"To your eternal discomfiture," he said, bowing ceremoniously. "May you go home and never come back! If you take Monsieur Blakeley with you, I hope you choke."

The lean man nodded gravely. "Prosit," he said. But the fat one leaned back and laughed consumedly.

Hotchkiss finished a mental synopsis of his position, and put down his glass. "Gentlemen," he said pompously, "within five minutes the man you want will be here, a murderer caught in a net of evidence so fine that a mosquito could not get through."

The detectives glanced at each other solemnly. Had they not in their possession a sealskin bag containing a wallet and a bit of gold chain, which, by putting the crime on me, would leave a gap big enough for Sullivan himself to crawl through?

"Why don't you say your little speech before Johnson brings the other man, Lawrence?" McKnight inquired. "They won't believe you, but it will help them to understand what is coming."

"You understand, of course," the lean man put in gravely, "that what you say may be used against you."

"I'll take the risk," I answered impatiently.

It took some time to tell the story of my worse than useless trip to Pittsburg, and its sequel. They listened gravely, without interruption.

"Mr. Hotchkiss here," I finished, "believes that the man Sullivan, whom we are momentarily expecting, committed the crime. Mr. McKnight is inclined to implicate Mrs. Conway, who stabbed Bronson and then herself last night. As for myself, I am open to conviction."

"I hope not," said the stout detective quizzically. And then Alison was announced. My impulse to go out and meet her was forestalled by the detectives, who rose when I did. McKnight, therefore, brought her in, and I met her at the door.

"I have put you to a great deal of trouble," I said contritely, when I saw her glance around the room. "I wish I had not—"

"It is only right that I should come," she replied, looking up at me. "I am the unconscious cause of most of it, I am afraid. Mrs. Dallas is going to wait in the outer office."

I presented Hotchkiss and the two detectives, who eyed her with interest. In her poise, her beauty, even in her gown, I fancy she represented a new type to them. They remained standing until she sat down.

"I have brought the necklace," she began, holding out a white-wrapped box, "as you asked me to."

I passed it, unopened, to the detectives. "The necklace from which was broken the fragment you found in the sealskin bag," I explained. "Miss West found it on the floor of the car, near lower ten."

"When did you find it?" asked the lean detective, bending forward.

"In the morning, not long before the wreck."

"Did you ever see it before?"

"I am not certain," she replied. "I have seen one very much like it." Her tone was troubled. She glanced at me as if for help, but I was powerless.

"Where?" The detective was watching her closely. At that moment there came an interruption. The door opened without ceremony, and Johnson ushered in a tall, blond man, a stranger to all of us: I glanced at Alison; she was pale, but composed and scornful. She met the new-comer's eyes full, and, caught unawares, he took a hasty backward step.

"Sit down, Mr. Sullivan," McKnight beamed cordially. "Have a cigar? I beg your pardon, Alison, do you mind this smoke?"

"Not at all," she said composedly. Sullivan had had a second to sound his bearings.

"No—no, thanks," he mumbled. "If you will be good enough to explain—"

"But that's what you're to do," McKnight said cheerfully, pulling up a chair. "You've got the most attentive audience you could ask. These two gentlemen are detectives from Pittsburg, and we are all curious to know the finer details of what happened on the car Ontario two weeks ago, the night your father-in-law was murdered." Sullivan gripped the arms of his chair. "We are not prejudiced, either. The gentlemen from Pittsburg are betting on Mr. Blakeley, over there. Mr. Hotchkiss, the gentleman by the radiator, is ready to place ten to one odds on you. And some of us have still other theories."

"Gentlemen," Sullivan said slowly, "I give you my word of honor that I did not kill Simon Harrington, and that I do not know who did."

"Fiddlededee!" cried Hotchkiss, bustling forward. "Why, I can tell you—" But McKnight pushed him firmly into a chair and held him there.

"I am ready to plead guilty to the larceny," Sullivan went on. "I took Mr. Blakeley's clothes, I admit. If I can reimburse him in any way for the inconvenience-"

The stout detective was listening with his mouth open. "Do you mean to say," he demanded, "that you got into Mr. Blakeley's berth, as he contends, took his clothes and forged notes, and left the train before the wreck?"

"Yes."

"The notes, then?"

"I gave them to Bronson yesterday. Much good they did him!" bitterly. We were all silent for a moment. The two detectives were adjusting themselves with difficulty to a new point of view; Sullivan was looking dejectedly at the floor, his hands hanging loose between his knees. I was watching Alison; from where I stood, behind her, I could almost touch the soft hair behind her ear.

"I have no intention of pressing any charge against you," I said with forced civility, for my hands were itching to get at him, "if you will give us a clear account of what happened on the Ontario that night."

Sullivan raised his handsome, haggard head and looked around at me. "I've seen you before, haven't I?" he asked. "Weren't you an uninvited guest at the Laurels a few days—or nights—ago? The cat, you remember, and the rug that slipped?"

"I remember," I said shortly. He glanced from me to Alison and quickly away.

"The truth can't hurt me," he said, "but it's devilish unpleasant. Alison, you know all this. You would better go out."

His use of her name crazed me. I stepped in front of her and stood over him. "You will not bring Miss West into the conversation," I threatened, "and she will stay if she wishes."

"Oh, very well," he said with assumed indifference. Hotchkiss just then escaped from Richey's grasp and crossed the room.

"Did you ever wear glasses?" he asked eagerly.

"Never." Sullivan glanced with some contempt at mine.

"I'd better begin by going back a little," he went on sullenly. "I suppose you know I was married to Ida Harrington about five years ago. She was a good girl, and I thought a lot of her. But her father opposed the marriage—he'd never liked me, and he refused to make any sort of settlement.

"I had thought, of course, that there would be money, and it was a bad day when I found out I'd made a mistake. My sister was wild with disappointment. We were pretty hard up, my sister and I."

I was watching Alison. Her hands were tightly clasped in her lap, and she was staring out of the window at the cheerless roof below. She had set her lips a little, but that was all.

"You understand, of course, that I'm not defending myself," went on the sullen voice. "The day came when old Harrington put us both out of the house at the point of a revolver, and I threatened—I suppose you know that, too—I threatened to kill him.

"My sister and I had hard times after that. We lived on the continent for a while. I was at Monte Carlo and she was in Italy. She met a young lady there, the granddaughter of a steel manufacturer and an heiress, and she sent for me. When I got to Rome the girl was gone. Last winter I was all in—social secretary to an Englishman, a wholesale grocer with a new title, but we had a row, and I came home. I went out to the Heaton boys' ranch in Wyoming, and met Bronson there. He lent me money, and I've been doing his dirty work ever since."

Sullivan got up then and walked slowly forward and back as he talked, his eyes on the faded pattern of the office rug.

"If you want to live in hell," he said savagely, "put yourself in another man's power. Bronson got into trouble, forging John Gilmore's name to those notes, and in some way he learned that a man was bringing the papers back to Washington on the Flier. He even learned the number of his berth, and the night before the wreck, just as I was boarding the train, I got a telegram."

Hotchkiss stepped forward once more importantly. "Which read, I think: 'Man with papers in lower ten, car seven. Get them.'"

Sullivan looked at the little man with sulky blue eyes.

"It was something like that, anyhow. But it was a nasty business, and it made matters worse that he didn't care that a telegram which must pass through a half dozen hands was more or less incriminating to me.

"Then, to add to the unpleasantness of my position, just after we boarded the train—I was accompanying my sister and this young lady, Miss West—a woman touched me on the sleeve, and I turned to face—my wife!

"That took away my last bit of nerve. I told my sister, and you can understand she was in a bad way, too. We knew what it meant. Ida had heard that I was going—"

He stopped and glanced uneasily at Alison.

"Go on," she said coldly. "It is too late to shield me. The time to have done that was when I was your guest."

"Well," he went on, his eyes turned carefully away from my face, which must have presented certainly anything but a pleasant sight. "Miss West was going to do me the honor to marry me, and—"

"You scoundrel!" I burst forth, thrusting past Alison West's chair. "You—you infernal cur!"

One of the detectives got up and stood between us. "You must remember, Mr. Blakeley, that you are forcing this story from this man. These details are unpleasant, but important. You were going to marry this young lady," he said, turning to Sullivan, "although you already had a wife living?"

"It was my sister's plan, and I was in a bad way for money. If I could marry, secretly, a wealthy girl and go to Europe, it was unlikely that Ida—that is, Mrs. Sullivan—would hear of it.

"So it was more than a shock to see my wife on the train, and to realize from her face that she knew what was going on. I don't know yet, unless some of the servants—well, never mind that.

"It meant that the whole thing had gone up. Old Harrington had carried a gun for me for years, and the same train wouldn't hold both of us. Of course, I thought that he was in the coach just behind ours."

Hotchkiss was leaning forward now, his eyes narrowed, his thin lips drawn to a line.

"Are you left-handed, Mr. Sullivan?" he asked.

Sullivan stopped in surprise.

"No," he said gruffly. "Can't do anything with my left hand." Hotchkiss subsided, crestfallen but alert. "I tore up that cursed telegram, but I was afraid to throw the scraps away. Then I looked around for lower ten. It was almost exactly across—my berth was lower seven, and it was, of course, a bit of exceptional luck for me that the car was number seven."

"Did you tell your sister of the telegram from Bronson?" I asked.

"No. It would do no good, and she was in a bad way without that to make her worse."

"Your sister was killed, think." The shorter detective took a small package from his pocket and held it in his hand, snapping the rubber band which held it.

"Yes, she was killed," Sullivan said soberly. "What I say now can do her no harm."

He stopped to push back the heavy hair which dropped over his forehead, and went on more connectedly.

"It was late, after midnight, and we went at once to our berths. I undressed, and then I lay there for an hour, wondering how I was going to get the notes. Some one in lower nine was restless and wide awake, but finally became quiet.

"The man in ten was sleeping heavily. I could hear his breathing, and it seemed to be only a question of getting across and behind the curtains of his berth without being seen. After that, it was a mere matter of quiet searching.

"The car became very still. I was about to try for the other berth, when some one brushed softly past, and I lay back again.

"Finally, however, when things had been quiet for a time, I got up, and after looking along the aisle, I slipped behind the curtains of lower ten. You understand, Mr. Blakeley, that I thought you were in lower ten, with the notes."

I nodded curtly.

"I'm not trying to defend myself," he went on. "I was ready to steal the notes—I had to. But murder!"

He wiped his forehead with his handkerchief.

"Well, I slipped across and behind the curtains. It was very still. The man in ten didn't move, although my heart was thumping until I thought he would hear it.

"I felt around cautiously. It was perfectly dark, and I came across a bit of chain, about as long as my finger. It seemed a queer thing to find there, and it was sticky, too."

He shuddered, and I could see Alison's hands clenching and unclenching with the strain.

"All at once it struck me that the man was strangely silent, and I think I lost my nerve. Anyhow, I drew the curtains open a little, and let the light fall on my hands. They were red, blood-red."

He leaned one hand on the back of the chair, and was silent for a moment, as though he lived over again the awful events of that more than awful night.

The stout detective had let his cigar go out; he was still drawing at it nervously. Richey had picked up a paper-weight and was tossing it from hand to hand; when it slipped and fell to the floor, a startled shudder passed through the room.

"There was something glittering in there," Sullivan resumed, "and on impulse I picked it up. Then I dropped the curtains and stumbled back to my own berth."

"Where you wiped your hands on the bed-clothing and stuck the dirk into the pillow." Hotchkiss was seeing his carefully built structure crumbling to pieces, and he looked chagrined.

"I suppose I did—I'm not very clear about what happened then. But when I rallied a little I saw a Russia leather wallet lying in the aisle almost at my feet, and, like a fool, I stuck it, with the bit of chain, into my bag.

"I sat there, shivering, for what seemed hours. It was still perfectly quiet, except for some one snoring. I thought that would drive me crazy.

"The more I thought of it the worse things looked. The telegram was the first thing against me—it would put the police on my track at once, when it was discovered that the man in lower ten had been killed.

"Then I remembered the notes, and I took out the wallet and opened it."

He stopped for a minute, as if the recalling of the next occurrence was almost beyond him.

"I took out the wallet," he said simply, "and opening it, held it to the light. In gilt letters was the name, Simon Harrington."

The detectives were leaning forward now, their eyes on his face.

"Things seemed to whirl around for a while. I sat there almost paralyzed, wondering what this new development meant for me.

"My wife, I knew, would swear I had killed her father; nobody would be likely to believe the truth.

"Do you believe me now?" He rooked around at us defiantly. "I am telling the absolute truth, and not one of you believes me!

"After a bit the man in lower nine got up and walked along the aisle toward the smoking compartment. I heard him go, and, leaning from my berth, watched him out of sight.

"It was then I got the idea of changing berths with him, getting into his clothes, and leaving the train. I give you my word I had no idea of throwing suspicion on him."

Alison looked scornfully incredulous, but I felt that the man was telling the truth.

"I changed the numbers of the berths, and it worked well. I got into the other man's berth, and he came back to mine. The rest was easy. I dressed in his clothes—luckily, they fitted—and jumped the train not far from Baltimore, just before the wreck."

"There is something else you must clear up," I said. "Why did you try to telephone me from M-, and why did you change your mind about the message?"

He looked astounded.

"You knew I was at M-?" he stammered.

"Yes, we traced you. What about the message?"

"Well, it was this way: of course, I did not know your name, Mr. Blakeley. The telegram said, 'Man with papers in lower ten, car seven,' and after I had made what I considered my escape, I began to think I had left the man in my berth in a bad way.

"He would probably be accused of the crime. So, although when the wreck occurred I supposed every one connected with the affair had been killed, there was a chance that you had survived. I've not been of much account, but I didn't want a man to swing because I'd left him in my place. Besides, I began to have a theory of my own.

"As we entered the car a tall, dark woman passed us, with a glass of water in her hand, and I vaguely remembered her. She was amazingly like Blanche Conway.

"If she, too, thought the man with the notes was in lower ten, it explained a lot, including that piece of a woman's necklace. She was a fury, Blanche Conway, capable of anything."

"Then why did you countermand that message?" I asked curiously.

"When I got to the Carter house, and got to bed—I had sprained my ankle in the jump—I went through the alligator bag I had taken from lower nine. When I found your name, I sent the first message. Then, soon after, I came across the notes. It seemed too good to be true, and I was crazy for fear the message had gone.

"At first I was going to send them to Bronson; then I began to see what the possession of the notes meant to me. It meant power over Bronson, money, influence, everything. He was a devil, that man."

"Well, he's at home now," said McKnight, and we were glad to laugh and relieve the tension.

Alison put her hand over her eyes, as if to shut out the sight of the man she had so nearly married, and I furtively touched one of the soft little curls that nestled at the back of her neck.

"When I was able to walk," went on the sullen voice, "I came at once to Washington. I tried to sell the notes to Bronson, but he was almost at the end of his rope. Not even my threat to send them back to you, Mr. Blakeley, could make him meet my figure. He didn't have the money."

McKnight was triumphant.

"I think you gentlemen will see reason in my theory now," he said. "Mrs. Conway wanted the notes to force a legal marriage, I suppose?"

"Yes."

The detective with the small package carefully rolled off the rubber band, and unwrapped it. I held my breath as he took out, first, the Russia leather wallet.

"These things, Mr. Blakeley, we found in the seal-skin bag Mr. Sullivan says he left you. This wallet, Mr. Sullivan—is this the one you found on the floor of the car?"

Sullivan opened it, and, glancing at the name inside, "Simon Harrington," nodded affirmatively.

"And this," went on the detective—"this is a piece of gold chain?"

"It seems to be," said Sullivan, recoiling at the blood-stained end.

"This, I believe, is the dagger." He held it up, and Alison gave a faint cry of astonishment and dismay. Sullivan's face grew ghastly, and he sat down weakly on the nearest chair.

The detective looked at him shrewdly, then at Alison's agitated face.

"Where have you seen this dagger before, young lady?" he asked, kindly enough.

"Oh, don't ask me!" she gasped breathlessly, her eyes turned on Sullivan. "It's—it's too terrible!"

"Tell him," I advised, leaning over to her. "It will be found out later, anyhow."

"Ask him," she said, nodding toward Sullivan. The detective unwrapped the small box Alison had brought, disclosing the trampled necklace and broken chain. With clumsy fingers he spread it on the table and fitted into place the bit of chain. There could be no doubt that it belonged there.

"Where did you find that chain?" Sullivan asked hoarsely, looking for the first time at Alison.

"On the floor, near the murdered man's berth."

"Now, Mr. Sullivan," said the detective civilly, "I believe you can tell us, in the light of these two exhibits, who really did murder Simon Harrington."

Sullivan looked again at the dagger, a sharp little bit of steel with a Florentine handle. Then he picked up the locket and pressed a hidden spring under one of the cameos. Inside, very neatly engraved, was the name and a date.

"Gentlemen," he said, his face ghastly, "it is of no use for me to attempt a denial. The dagger and necklace belonged to my sister, Alice Curtis!"

Chapter 31

AND ONLY ONE ARM

Hotchkiss was the first to break the tension.

"Mr. Sullivan," he asked suddenly, "was your sister left-handed?"

"Yes."

· Hotchkiss put away his note-book and looked around with an air of triumphant vindication. It gave us a chance to smile and look relieved. After all, Mrs. Curtis was dead. It was the happiest solution of the unhappy affair. McKnight brought Sullivan some whisky, and he braced up a little.

"I learned through the papers that my wife was in a Baltimore hospital, and yesterday I ventured there to see her. I felt if she would help me to keep straight, that now, with her father and my sister both dead, we might be happy together.

"I understand now what puzzled me then. It seemed that my sister went into the next car and tried to make my wife promise not to interfere. But Ida—Mrs. Sullivan—was firm, of course. She said her father had papers, certificates and so on, that would stop the marriage at once.

"She said, also, that her father was in our car, and that there would be the mischief to pay in the morning. It was probably when my sister tried to get the papers that he awakened, and she had to do—what she did."

It was over. Save for a technicality or two, I was a free man. Alison rose quietly and prepared to go; the men stood to let her pass, save Sullivan who sat crouched in his chair, his face buried in his hands. Hotchkiss, who had been tapping the desk with his pencil, looked up abruptly and pointed the pencil at me.

"If all this is true, and I believe it is,—then who was in the house next door, Blakeley, the night you and Mr. Johnson searched? You remember, you said it was a woman's hand at the trap door."

I glanced hastily at Johnson, whose face was impassive. He had his hand on the knob of the door and he opened it before he spoke.

"There were a number of scratches on Mrs. Conway's right hand," he observed to the room in general. "Her wrist was bandaged and badly bruised."

He went out then, but he turned as he closed the door and threw at me a glance of half-amused, half-contemptuous tolerance.

McKnight saw Alison, with Mrs. Dallas, to their carriage, and came back again. The gathering in the office was breaking up. Sullivan, looking worn and old, was standing by the window, staring at the broken necklace in his hand. When he saw me watching him, he put it on the desk and picked up his hat.

"If I can not do anything more—" he hesitated.

"I think you have done about enough," I replied grimly, and he went out.

I believe that Richey and Hotchkiss led me somewhere to dinner, and that, for fear I would be lonely without him, they sent for Johnson. And I recall a spirited discussion in which Hotchkiss told the detective that he could manage certain cases, but that he lacked induction. Richey and I were mainly silent. My thoughts would slip ahead to that hour, later in the evening, when I should see Alison again.

I dressed in savage haste finally, and was so particular about my tie that Mrs. Klopton gave up in despair.

"I wish, until your arm is better, that you would buy the kind that hooks on," she protested, almost tearfully. "I'm sure they look very nice, Mr. Lawrence. My late husband always—"

"That's a lover's knot you've tied this time," I snarled, and, jerking open the bow knot she had so painfully executed, looked out the window for Johnson—until I recalled that he no longer belonged in my perspective. I ended by driving frantically to the club and getting George to do it.

I was late, of course. The drawing-room and library at the Dallas home were empty. I could hear billiard balls rolling somewhere, and I turned the other way. I found Alison at last on the balcony, sitting much as she had that night on the beach,—her chin in her hands, her eyes fixed unseeingly on the trees and lights of the square across. She was even whistling a little, softly. But this time the plaintiveness was gone. It was a tender little tune. She did not move, as I stood beside her, looking down. And now, when the moment had come, all the thousand and one things I had been waiting to say forsook me, precipitately beat a retreat, and left me unsupported. The arc-moon sent little fugitive lights over her hair, her eyes, her gown.

"Don't—do that," I said unsteadily. "You—you know what I want to do when you whistle!"

She glanced up at me, and she did not stop. She did not stop! She went on whistling softly, a bit tremulously. And straightway I forgot the street, the chance of passers-by, the voices in the house behind us. "The world doesn't hold any one but you," I said reverently. "It is our world, sweetheart. I love you."

And I kissed her.

A boy was whistling on the pavement below. I let her go reluctantly and sat back where I could see her.

"I haven't done this the way I intended to at all," I confessed. "In books they get things all settled, and then kiss the lady."

"Settled?" she inquired.

"Oh, about getting married and that sort of thing," I explained with elaborate carelessness. "We—we could go down to Bermuda—or—or Jamaica, say in December."

She drew her hand away and faced me squarely.

"I believe you are afraid!" she declared. "I refuse to marry you unless you propose properly. Everybody does it. And it is a woman's privilege: she wants to have that to look back to."

"Very well," I consented with an exaggerated sigh. "If you will promise not to think I look like an idiot, I shall do it, knee and all."

I had to pass her to close the door behind us, but when I kissed her again she protested that we were not really engaged.

I turned to look down at her. "It is a terrible thing," I said exultantly, "to love a girl the way I love you, and to have only one arm!" Then I closed the door.

From across the street there came a sharp crescendo whistle, and a vaguely familiar figure separated itself from the park railing.

"Say," he called, in a hoarse whisper, "shall I throw the key down the elevator shaft?"

Made in the USA
Middletown, DE
28 September 2018